How My Prank Stories In
Social Media Web Sites
Got Me Committed In The
Psychiatric Ward At Bellevue Hospital

Do I have another story for you, and you girls better tie a knot on your bloomers and you guys hold on to your toupees, because I'm gonna blow them away!!!

I warned you I'd be back but this time bigger and better

Still the best of the best since the invention of slice bread and pockets on 'T' shirts

He's been called by some one of the greatest story tellers that ever lived. There's nothing he can't do or won't try. He's done it all, from being a graveyard digger, to a tightrope walker, and it's all because he isn't afraid to reinvent himself. Sit back and take a lesson from the old guy, yep the new kid on the block, who will out smart you and leave you laughing in stitches

I'll paint your toe nails, you paint my toe nails, then we'll paint up the town red!!!

Added Bonus;
Cyber Comedy, The Jimmy And Marisol Story

How My Prank Stories In
Social Media Web Sites
Got Me Committed In The
Psychiatric Ward At Bellevue Hospital

JIMMY CORREA

iUniverse, Inc.
Bloomington

How My Prank Stories In Social Media Web Sites Got Me Committed In The Psychiatric Ward At Bellevue Hospital

iUniverse books may be ordered through booksellers or by contacting:

iUniverse
1663 Liberty Drive
Bloomington, IN 47403
www.iuniverse.com
1-800-Authors (1-800-288-4677)

ISBN: 978-1-4759-7510-9 (sc)
ISBN: 978-1-4759-7511-6 (ebk)

Printed in the United States of America

iUniverse rev. date: 03/14/2013

Contents

Dedicated to my children,

John James Chris & Luisa

My Acknowledgment

Well there are so many people I would like to thank. But in all honesty, it's the web sites that deserve all the credit because without them I would never have been able to communicate, and build a rapport with all my friends past and present. Also I must give a shout out to one special gal, my friend Marisol. Yes that crazy girl from the other side of the pond, who has brightened up my life and made me laugh throughout the making of the second half of this book. When are we going to actually meet? Well that depends, maybe when this book becomes a best seller or some crazy producer, a la Mel Brooks, Rob Reiner, Ron Howard, Steven Spielberg, Penny Marshall, Quentin Tarantino or Tyler Perry turns our story into a TV series or a blockbuster movie and not until then. Who knows? I'm sure when Lucy met Ricky; she didn't realize what they had and what it made of them; one of the world's greatest comedy duo of all time. I hope you laugh as much as I did, and still do every time I pick up this book. I just can't stop laughing! I might even buy five copies for my mother. Enjoy and thank you, thank you, thank you, and please do come back you hear, Jimmy!!!

Introduction

I don't recall if it was Charlie Chaplin, Jerry Lewis, Martin Lawrence, Cher or my good friend Whipsy who once said that laughter is the best medicine to cure whatever ails you. So here's a dose of that. If you don't laugh your ass off, I will eat my hat in a Macy's store window. Well for your information this is a continuation of my previous book 'How My Prank Stories In 'You Tube' Made Me An Overnight Sensation.' This time I've expanded and lucky for me no one has made any derogatory remarks to any of my stories. Oh, that happens every day, on You Tube and Facebook. Just look at the comments people leave behind to videos, photos, movies, or songs. So I guess Ricky Nelson, that great philosopher of the 20th century, who said "you can't please everyone so you got to please yourself" was right on the money.

Friends of mine say I should do standup comedy. Are they crazy? I would die in a heartbeat, and besides my insurance policy keeps lapsing every other month. My heirs would get diddly squat, other than that Social Security allotment of 250 dollars they give you, and that's not nearly enough for a simple cremation. And honestly speaking, who do you know in their right mind wants to hear a Puerto Rican/American lecture them about the facts of life? Yes this is a compilation of my facts of life. I tell stories of my youth, my school days, and my time spent on the streets of NYC diddy bopping, playing skellies, or hop scotch with the girls. Also I reveal tidbits of my first love affairs, and even later of my work places. What work places? Glad you asked! When I worked at a brokerage firm down in Wall Street, buying and selling all types of shit, stocks, bonds, commodities, options, annuities, treasuries, derivatives, money markets, cd's, futures, currencies, and all the toxic junk they had to offer. And also my brief tenure at the ING Service Center in Minot ND making beneficiary changes, addresses changes, adding child riders, and collateral assignments. But that's not all, during my lunch breaks you would find me chasing beaver, the two legged kind, don't ask, and rabbits and deer for dinner. Now in my current tour of duty as we speak I work at a local Home Depot Store, here in NYC, where they got me selling nipples and ball cocks in the plumbing aisles. My mother would kill me if she knew. But then that's where I have my opportunity to be on stage, and hone my skills as a story teller. Sometimes the customers would walk away scratching their heads saying, "that freaking boy is crazy, who the heck let him out of the psychiatric ward?"

Hey, don't laugh! Many of them come back looking for me to tell them some more revelations. So who's the crazy one? And that's when I knew I should start charging a fee for my services. I would tell them of my arm transplant therefore the reason I was wearing long sleeve shirts in the dead of summer because I didn't want anybody to notice I had received a woman's arm. Why it was five inches shorter, smoother, hairless, and prettier than the other. Or the time a NYC Fire Department ambulance driver nearly pushed me off the road because he had a whole bunch of toes to deliver. Oh, you don't want to know! Or that dispute I had with a lady bus driver because she called me a moron. oooooooh, I wanted to beat her with my shoe! Well it's all here and much more. So sit back, get comfortable, get you a beer, or whatever that floats your boat and find out what more I have to say. You might choke on that beef jerky we sell at the store. You might even pee on yourself laughing so hard. But then that's the risk you'll have to take. Like I always say, "no tickie, no shirtie." Well not me per say, my China Man at the laundry place where I hang trying to pick up babes. Ok ok where I hang. Take care and god bless and say a little prayer for me. I can surely use all the help I can get. Oh, it's time for my encore; don't wait up the queen of talk is here. No not Cher, Oprah. Oprah who, Oprah Winfrey Oprah that Oprah!!! Ciao Jimmy, aka Mr. Stand Up, I wish!!!

What is Social Media

Social Media is an assortment of internet web sites that enhance the sharing of information, text, photos, audio, and video. It allows people to share as much or as little information as they like. There are literally hundreds if not thousands of social media web sites and that includes those dating match sites, games, art clubs, etc. You name it, it's probably there. My prank stories have been posted and viewed in the following sites: Classmates, Facebook, and You Tube. Soon on Twitter, Flickr and a bunch of other blogging sites. But that's for another time and maybe another book—who knows.

Classmates.com was created to assist members in finding friends and classmates from kindergarten, mid school, high school, college, and work places. You also have the opportunity to view and buy high school yearbooks if available. One can post videos, movie trailers, music tracks, and photographic images. It is estimated there are 50 million members, but only about 4 million are paid subscribers. It is open to people from the ages of 18 on up and free for people to register as a <u>basic</u> member with limited functions. Or as a <u>Gold</u> member who pay a fee, and have unlimited access to view other members' profiles, photos, biographies, timelines, interests, announcements, and to send and receive emails from any member.

Facebook is a popular site that allows its members to communicate, connect and engage with each other's common interests and groups. It is the by far the largest social network in the world where one can view and share photos, videos, and blogs. It presently has 1,000,000,000 members and is open to people from the age of 13 and older.

You Tube is a website in which users can upload, view and share videos including movie clips, TV clips, music videos, as well as amateur video blogging, short original videos, and educational videos. Most of the content on YouTube has been uploaded by individuals, and big media corporations including CBS, the BBC, VEVO to name just a few. Unregistered users can watch videos, while registered users can upload an unlimited number of videos. It is estimated the site has over eight hundred million users a month and ranks as the third most visited website on the Internet, behind Google and Facebook.

Yes it's true my crazy stories got me committed to the psychiatric ward at Bellevue Hospital. You can find me right in front of the nurses' station because they consider me dangerous to others, to myself, and to the rats that roam that there building and if I do get out of hand they can easily zap me, ouch. The address is: 462 1st Avenue, New York, NY 10016 in case you want to pay me a visit. But let me warn you, you think I'm crazy, the whole gangs there, Peter Pan, Wild Bill Hickok, Peggy Sue, aka the notorious axe murderer, and Josie 'Freaking' Wales, the hang 'em high ring leader and her side kick Gloria, well she aint Marie. Oh, let's not leave out Angel Vee, the mercy of death psychopath with the four split personalities. Today she's the first lady, Mary Todd Lincoln, well I did say they were nuts but who's judging who, we're all nuts living in a far out world. The building is meant for short-term care; but they want me there for life, seems I scam the patients out of their cigarettes with three card monti, but let's not go there, they claim I cheat. Hey, they're the ones who are picking the cards you freaking moron. So don't be a stranger visit me when you need a friend and I can surely use a hug or two. Ciao and how Jimmy, the nut job or should I say the nut cracker!!!!

In America we have a tradition that on every October 31st we get to act silly for the day, it's called Halloween. Well I have a story that will shock you, this year I got dressed up as a 'Streaker' or should I say dressed down. So here I am with not a stitch of clothing on, on my way to a party when before you could say "how's it hanging" a crowd developed and they were so impressed that they decided to join me. After an hour or so we were arrested for indecent exposure. The NYPD stopped us, frisked us, what for there was nothing to check, we were all buck naked. They threw us in a paddy wagon and hauled our asses to night court. When it was my turn to speak up in my defense and as the so called ring leader I told the judge I was on my way to The Freaker's Ball when the crowd of about 100 joined me and we roamed the streets hooting and hollering all dressed in our birthday suits. I reminded her "this is America baby, the land of the free and I can do whatever I want to do." So I removed my robe and you should have seen by the expression on her face she was aroused and said in stuttering words 'not not in my my court. I was sentenced to do 100 hours of community service and fined twenty-five dollars. Later she came down to the lockup pen and wished me luck, sure she did just wanted to see me/it again. I knew what she was up to so I dropped my robe so she could get another look, that horny toad. We switched phone #'s and addresses, she said she could give me some legal pointers, hahaha

sure then I'll have to tip her, don't ask. I'm going to take this to the Supreme Courts, what say you is this a tradition in your neck of the woods, Halloween, ciao, Jimmy.
Dr. Hook—Freakin' At The Freaker's Ball

Folks my friend who will remain anonymous told me how she gave Jerry Lee Lewis the idea for his big hit 'Great Balls Of Fire.' When she was a little girl her mum and dad bought her a pony, a strawberry-roan foal, he was beautiful and it broke her heart when they had to have him gelded. I being a city slickster didn't know what gelding was until she explained that's when you remove the stallion's testicles. That night they had a roaring bonfire and the vet's assistant threw the pony's balls into the fire. Her pony never forgave her, hey I didn't know ponies can talk but what do I know, like I said I'm all city. If you look at the bright side it made a star out of Jerry Lee Lewis cos he got wind of the story and that's when he penned that song 'Great Balls Of Fire.' Thanks Susie for sharing that wonderful story and I hope it's still in your barn and rides you all over London town, in the meantime folks enjoy the song, ciao Jimmy
Jerry Lee Lewis—Great Balls Of Fire

Last week I was doing some landscaping in my back yard when I accidentally hit a gold mine, yep I discovered oil. I was so excited I called my boss and told him what he could do with my job; yep shove it where it don't shine. A week later I got a huge bill from my oil company that I owed them a ton of money and here I am putting that gushing oil into them giant oil cans, one hundred and forty to be exact. That's when I realized I didn't hit pay dirt, I cracked into their oil lines and now I got to beg my boss for forgiveness so I can get my job back. I'm so ashamed but I know how to butter him up, take him out for lunch at the 'all you can eat sushi bar' and pop him the question. Might have to take him to the girlie bar too if I know him, that freaking horny toad, ciao got to go and beg for mercy, bye Jimmy
Chuck Jackson—Beg Me

Folks I got a question, can you love somebody you never met, well I think I am in love with such a woman and I don't know if it's just my hormones running wild or my heart just skipping a beat. You see when I think of her or when we start chatting I go bonkers. Heck, I don't know everything about her. I've known her for over two years on and off and I think she is everything a man could possibly want. What first attracted me were her sweet charms and the beautiful poetry that she recited to me and when she told me funny stories than I was hooked line and sinker. Within time it reached that next level and you just knew it would lead to that final encounter. What final encounter, when I'm face to face and looking into her eyes you just know I'll be able to see deep into her soul. Omg what should I do! Drop everything and high tail it to her house and sweep her off her feet. Oh please give me a sign. I don't know what to do in the meantime I dedicate this playlist currently featured on my channel to her and maybe she'll get the hint and throw me a life raft. Without it I'm going to sink and disappear once and for all, broken hearted is more like it. Thanks for your time and wish me luck, Jimmy!!!
A Night of Ecstasy At Dakota Jim's Sock Hop 1 (Playlist)

Folks this new year, 2013, I'm turning a new leaf, yep I'm going to have a few cosmetic improvements, a tummy tuck, a butt job, and a face lift. Why you ask, because

I want to look my best when I win all those awards for all my accomplishments. What accomplishments, I see you don't read the tabloids or patronize in book stores, must be you got deep pockets and short arms. Well enough of you, I'm going to have my star on that Hollywood Walk-A-Fame and win Pulitzers and that Porno Star of the Year statue. Yes my acting debut in 'Jimmy Does Mrs. Chatterley' was my coming out, and I can't wait till I do 'The Spanish Patient.' You talk about leaning her against the wall, try in the halls, in the floor, and up on the roof. Thank you and don't forget my newest book 'How I Became a Porno Star in You Tube' will mesmerize you to say the least, ciao, Jimmy, Mr. Wonderful!! Eric Burdon And War—Spill The Wine

The three most important things in life for me are: one, my health, two, a feisty woman, and three, how much money I got in my pockets. So when you see me coming down the street with a smile on my face and my pockets bulging, yes most of those bulges are wads and wads and wads of money. That other bulge, don't ask but it's true I'm so happy to see you. My daddy once said you can move mountains, walk on water, and never ever have to kiss ass ever again if you got that green stuff and I aint talking about cabbage or spinach. The more you got the more power you got. Well this song is all me, yes you got that right, cos that's all I want too, money, lots of it. It will make me happier than a pig in slop and if you want some of this you got to give me all of that and some of that, all your money, and then some of the goodies. Like I always say no tickie, no shirtie, Jimmy the money man

Ps
You can still buy my book, 'How My Prank Stories In 'You Tube' Made Me An Overnight Sensation' at any Barnes and Noble or through amazon.com or my publisher iUniverse.com
Barrett Strong—Money (That's What I Want)

My fortune teller says I got the makings of a 'black magic man.' I don't know about no magic man and definitely not black but I know I have uncanny abilities. If you mess with me I'll take a Polish pickle and stick it where it doesn't shine, yep, up your butt. And if you try to cheat me I'll feed you some zombie nuts for dinner, she was right I'm not only crazy but lovable, ciao, Jimmy
Santana—Black Magic Woman

Folks I'm writing a book on the subject of love making, you know, how I became a ladies man and how I always get what I want. This would be more beneficial to marriage counselors or those who are frustrated cos they aint getting any, any what, pudding pie. It would be an excellent handy book where I can reveal my techniques in love making. It will make 'The Joy of Sex' book so out dated. It will show you the proper method to taking a girl up to your house for a night cap. Explain to you the steps from posting that "do not disturb, gone fishing" sign on your door to that point where your body can't pop, yes too pooped to pop. So don't bother to call, my phone lines will be disconnected and if you hear fire alarms don't panic it's only me fighting fire with fire and disregard the hooting and hollering we're getting down and dirty, dirty dancing that is. Well I don't need to draw you any pictures do I, just buy the book when it comes out. I must warn you it might have parts 2, 3, and 4 and the photos might be too revealing but that's a bonus for you just out of the box, again no pun intended. Who knows I might make an encyclopedia out of it. Tell me

what you think or if you have any questions you would like me to answer, ciao, Jimmy, the Love Hunk . . .
All 4 One—I Can Love You Like That

Here's a reply from my friend, Mz. Bea Hayvin, whose identity will remain anonymous as well!

Don't make it too LONG, or too THICK, and not a HARD back either . . . hahaha and not a BIG introduction either, just lots of little volumes to get down to the nitty gritty. Better still put it on a kindle with a night light for under the covers . . . Nobody wants to have to wade through 15 chapters and 400 pages to get to the part they want to get to, hahaha

And spell it out with pictures puh-lease especially for those men, (not as experienced as you are) who have no efffing clue around a woman's anatomy and think that the horizontal hokey pokey in out in out and shake it all about is enough hahaha

Us women have waited a long time for this book. I guarantee you it'll enter the best seller list, and easily SQUEEZE into the numero uno spot and BLOWWWW all the others books outa the water and it'll be a huge SUCKcess even though I know there will be STIFF competition.
Glad you got the BALLS to do it.
Mz. Bea Hayvin

The two worst things in life is a nagging woman and a farting horse. You see this guy is getting ready to get romantic with his lady love, and then the horse blows it for him, yep right into her face. Ooooopps I would hate to be either one of them. Let me see him kiss her now hahahaha . . .
Bud Light Commercial—Horse Farts in Girl's Face!

When somebody tells you, "You Aint Seen Nothing Yet," you just know you're in for a big surprise. The love making becomes so good you start out slowly and work up a frenzy that you think you've just died and went to heaven. Yeah heaven is the primary destination, a journey that will take us around the world, don't ask hahaha. Bye bye, so long, she's showing me her trophies and attributes whatever the heck that is, hahaha.
Jimmy
BTO—You Ain't Seen Nothing Yet

Folks I'm taking care of business and there's a whole lot of over time going on, how so. I'm the new proud owner of 'Jimmy's Bootlegging On-The-Go.' You see there's a lot of money to be made in the manufacturing of liquor, so I'm going into that money making business, called bootlegging. I'm going to make all kinds of liquor, scotch, whiskey, rum, Piña Coladas, tequila, and Jimmy Changas. And btw don't be fooled I always thought scotch came from Scotland, no way buster; you can easily make it in your own bath tub. But you aint heard the best of it, I throw in a special ingredient and you be growing hair, sometimes in the wrong places but I have no control over that. Where I really want it to grow is on my head but in some cases it grows in between your toes, or on your knee caps, or under your under arms and that aint too pretty. Now, if I could only make it grow in the right spots I'd be making triple the amount of money I'm making now. No, I'm not complaining cos I mingle with the crème de la crème hotties, that's them in the video taking care of business, yeah me, hahaha. Hey you single girls out there are you looking for some action I can use another hottie, or two. Just forward me your credentials, you know, your height, weight, measurements, and what is it that you're good at, in other words your specialty, might be able to use you if you play your cards right and the whole nine yards, byeeeeeeee Jimmy BTO (Bachman Turner Overdrive)—Takin' Care Of Business

I once lived in a mid-western town called Minot located in the great state of North Dakota home of the *HØSTFEST come every October. Well Minot has horses and cows up to the yang yang, yep one heck of a messy town. There's so much manure you have to watch your step every which way you go. They say when you step in a pile of shit it's good luck, well you can keep that kind of good luck, I want no part of it, leave me out of it. It's not only nasty but it stinks. I did notice nobody bothers you or comes near you, so back to my original story. I would hang in them there cowboy bars and whenever I could spit and mount them mechanical bulls. Soon I was the best bronco buster in the bar. My fame soon spread for miles, people would come from all over just to watch see me manhandle that bucket of bolts. Every weekend they would put up a contest to see who could beat me, the betting got so out of hand even the Vegas boys would get in on the action. I'm now called the Evel Knievel of bull riding, can't wait till I move it up a notch, yeah I'm only on level two, and there's eight more to go. You aint seen nothing yet, well it's time to go, a bus load of girls just got in, got to show them what I've got, no not that, my riding skills, hahahahaha, bye and happy trails to you all, and do come back you hear!!!
Bachman Turner Overdrive—You Aint Seen Nothing Yet

I've notice that in the winter months the blood banks are always looking for some good men and women; they're looking for some fresh blood and they try to lure you in with a promise of a T-shirt or a button. But every time I give some I have to be blindfolded, you see I can't stand the sight of blood. I have this fear I'm going to bleed out. It's for a good cause and another good cause is donating your body parts so others may live. So carry your drivers ID and sign that donor card section that allows them to harvest your organs for transplants, thanks Jimmy

Ps
I got me an arm transplant; it's a long story, tell you about it some other time

Some words of wisdom that I always like sharing. Two years ago a friend of mind was not responding to my e-mail shares, so I asked her what was the matter and she said her boyfriend left her for another. I reminded her about the boy who was crying because he wanted a brand new pair of shoes but what about the amputee who has no feet or the homeless man who has no place to call his own. Who has to go through the dumpster looking for leftover food. Or what about those children born with a cleft pallet or blind. So forget that loser and know there are plenty good fish in the sea. In fact that fella really did you a favor; he showed he didn't love you so get yourself a real barracuda. Go take a vacation, meet up with some family members or friends and time will heal, believe me it always does. Well my message hit home she wrote me back saying as she read my reply

she was crying because everything I had said was the truth and it woke her up. She's still in YT and makes some of the best videos around, her viewing stats are awesome, thanks and I hope I reached into your hearts too. Peace and love, Jimmy
The Marvelettes—Too Many Fish In The Sea

Sometimes I wake up and say to myself what is it that I can do today to give something back to the world. Well I'm no rocket scientist or brain surgeon but if I can make a comment that will have you laughing right out of your chair and onto the floor. That's worth any medicine I could possibly prescribe. Hope today you laugh your ass off like nobody is watching you or is it dance like nobody is watching you, well whatever makes you happy happy, ciao Jimmy

Folks let me ask you a question is it just me and Eric Clapton but why is it that when you're doing well, you know, got a lot of spending loot from an inheritance, or from winning at the ponies, or hitting the lotto everybody seems to know your name. They even want to be your long lost friend, or your lover and they can't compliment you enough. They even drop by your house day and night, 24/7 to break bread and drink whatever you've got to drink but the minute your chips are down or the booze runs dry nobody but nobody wants to know you. All of a sudden you're like the plague. Well when I do get back on my feet again I'm going to do what that Sinatra fella did, roll myself up in a balloon and fly. Might even book a ticket and split this here town for good because I'm going to get me some real down to earth friends, know any. Send them my way, those with some spending loot, looking for a real man, yep me. Thanks and don't call me, I'll call you, Jimmy
Eric Clapton—Nobody Knows You When You're Down And Out

Folks these are words of wisdom that I live by and want to share them with you all. My mother always said, put on some clean underwear because you never know when you might end up in a hospital. Now my daddy on the other hand said, you never know what hottie you might end up picking up. Bless them both, they were smart alrighty so do as I say and not as I do, well you get the idea, I hope, Jimmy

. . . yes, knock her down and she's only going to get up and you don't want to know what she's capable of doing. If I were you better get out of town because there's going to be a massacre all right, but don't take my word see for yourself. Just tell me where to send your remains cos she's going to fire away. Yeah, fire away and Pat Benatar my favorite female rocker of all time knows too well how to fire away. If you ever get a chance go to one of her concerts and you too will be blown away!!!
Pat Benatar—Hit Me With Your Best Shot

Anybody who knows me knows this movie would make the list as one of my most inspirational movies of all time. It's Henry Fonda portraying 'Young Abe Lincoln,' and in this dramatic yet comical scene Abe is trying to protect a potential client/s out of being hanged by an angry drunken lynch mob. It is so inspiring it will knock your socks off, always does to me, no wonder I'm missing a bunch of socks and so will you, enjoy and tell me I was right, Jimmy
Henry Fonda—Young Abe Lincoln

"Cool Hand Luke" starring the incomparable Paul Newman was another big classic inspirational movie of mine, and yes they weren't in sync. They had a failure to communicate because all Luke wanted to do was run and run, it even killed him. Enjoy and do see the movie in its entirety, ciao Jimmy

Paul Newman—Cool Hand Luke (Failure to Communicate)

Folks there's a new sheriff in town, that's me in my avatar, so don't think cos we're friends that you can come into my town and start a ruckus. I will arrest you without blinking an eye. Jimmy, the new sheriff of da Eu Es of Aye and yes I'm badder than Jim Croce, Leroy Brown, or ole King Kong. Oh how I miss that boy, Jim Croce, the lord took him away from us way too soon. My guess he's up there entertaining all his predecessors and those that came after, showing them the proper way to tell a story. A story that will not only put a smile on their faces, but teach them the true values in life. Though gone his memory and legacy will long live on, thanks the other Jim, me!!!

Jim Croce—Bad, Bad Leroy Brown

Guys I need to know have any of you ever received a "Dear John Letter." That's a letter a woman who has no 'cojones' sends to a man that their relationship is over, finished, finite can't make it any more plainer than that. Well if you were that John fella know it could end your world. The TV series is based on a group of misfits who meet to discuss their failures in life and in hopes to put their lives back in some kind of order. I was once a member of such a group, we conspired on how to get even with our spouses and even thought of burning their houses down to the ground, but that's for another time, another story. We did a lot of things together, joined nudist clubs, and partied till we were drunk, or got over on our dates hahaha. Can't say no more because I was one little devil, ok, ok one mean cold callus conniving devil, ciao Jimmy

Dear John—TV sitcom

pt. 1

pt. 2

Fyi, 'Dear John' was a popular TV series in 1988 through 1992 starring Judd Hirsch who joins the One-2-One Club, a group for divorced, widowed, or lonely souls. The group is led by Louise, a British woman. Other members include Kate, a divorcée; Kirk an obnoxious ladies' man; Ralph, a neurotic tollbooth collector; Bonnie, a feisty senior citizen; Tom, her boyfriend; and Mary Beth, a former Southern belle. Every cast member was superb but Kirk did steal the show quite often, I would laugh in tears, hope it brings you fond memories, thanks Jimmy

Dear John—TV sitcom

Here's a copy of my <u>current </u>resume taken from my YT channel, theloveman11378, no job too small or too big I won't tackle even if it kills you:

Author, gravedigger, prize fighter, military man, private dick, fire fighter, repo man, bank robber, hit man, singer, drummer, trapeze artist, tightrope walker, con man, ventriloquist, tango, mambo, and meringue instructor, secret agent man, midget wrestler, rapper, bass man, professional auditioner, mooner for hire, miner for gold, wheeler/dealer, organ stealer, pole dancer, cowboy, counterfeiter, American Idol wannabe, a hunk, shoe shine boy, a contender, a Chippendale dancer for money, ass kisser, scam artist, chef, a streaker, a bag of chips, Twinkies, ho ho's, scooter pie, gummy bears all rolled into one, your man, and whatever else you want me to be . . .

Yes I've done it all, not too proud of everything I've done but then you know if at first you don't succeed try and try and try again. I've tried so many things I don't know if I'm coming or going or going in circles. Well it's true cos if Christopher Columbus hadn't tried we'd still be the stone ages and King George the 31st would be sucking us dry of more tea taxes and Ray Charles would have never been discovered. What have I've contributed to society, well besides pockets on T-shirts, mambo no. 6, the hoola-hoop, the double-dutch jump rope and now my exotic recipes is starting to take off. I've got over 100 patents but it's not necessary to name them all. Even got an idea for a movie pilot about a mask woman who has a horse and a side kick named Pronto cos he does everything fast, damn is he fast on the draw byeeeeeee
Jimmy, aka Mr. Kimosabe
Flip Wilson—Christopher Columbus

Can I tell you a secret, I'm a natural born scam artist I pretend to be a long lost orphan and when I find a prospective sucker I tell them I hired a private dick to find the parents who abandoned me at birth and you're it. How's it going, well so far I haven't had any luck, one time I told this lady that she was my mother and she died right there and then didn't even give me a chance to have her sign all the papers necessary to inherit her estate. Oh well I'll keep trying till I succeed, you know what PT Barnum once said, "there's a sucker born every minute", now if I could only locate a handful I'd be in the money. Hey, do you know any, I can cut you in on the deal, how's 10% sound to you, ok ok 20%, take it or leave it, my daddy once said 20 of something is better than 20 of nothing. Keep me posted and mums the word don't need anybody cutting in on my brilliant idea, ok idea, ciao Jimmy
The Shields—You Cheated

Hey, now you can add 'chef' to my already highly decorated resume, it started two months ago when I was in YT desperately trying to pick up some pointers on the art of cooking. Well I did say desperate, YT must be good for something. You see I like to experiment and I came up with some wild crazy exotic food recipe inventions. What, you don't believe me well here are a few of my inventions: Wild Rooster Mango, Upside Down Turtle Legs Casserole, Peacock A La King, Pigeon On A Canopy with a side order of rice and beans, oh I can go on and on. But I must be honest it really started twelve years ago when I did my lay over at the Rahway State Prison for that botched bank heist. Yes I got caught and sentenced to eleven years where as my side kick only got sixty days. Why's that, because they thought she was too old to go to the pokey. Too old my foot, she's the one who raised me and she should have done those eleven years not I. Who was she, my grandmother Aluisa who fell asleep at the wheel of our getaway car? Well any way I took up cooking in prison and in no time became head chef after my two superiors mysteriously came down with toe main poisoning, they never caught the culprit but I rather we change the subject. Hey, if any of you folks, especially you sexy gals in YT land would be so kind to send me some of your recipes or want to get together I will be more than honored "**Maybe**" even

post your name and your status for being a good do be. Btw you want that toe main recipe, send me a self-addressed envelope where you could be located and who it is you want out of your misery. Thanks again and don't feel bad you too can be anything you want just have to have 'cojones' and a whole bunch of desires. Got to go, going to make pastrami on a bed of snake casserole on a whole wheat bun, umm umm umm, yeah starting to eat healthy in case I do hook up with some babes from YT!!!
The Chantels—Maybe

Here's a release of a previous true incident that happened to me a few years ago:
Folks I got a story you just aint going to believe, I was involved in a car accident that had my arm barely hanging on a string. The good news was that a lady had just died and they were harvesting all her organs and body parts and they were considering giving me an arm transplant the first of its kind. The only drawback was that it was a lady's and her arm was a lot shorter, five inches to be exact, and smoother than a baby's butt, and hairless like you don't need a Brazilian waxing at my barbershop. So I went ahead after some arm twisting and they performed that 135 hour, 45 doctor assisted surgery without a hitch. A few weeks later on a follow up visit the doctor asked me did I have any problems and I said "yes, only one, every time I go to pee her hand won't let go," hahaha, enjoy this Roy Hamilton song and do think of me every time you hear "Don't Let Go" or have to pee, ciao Jimmy

I get a lot of compliments but the best one of all is when somebody, girls that is, call me a saxy thing, thank you, I am. When I was frolicking on the beaches of Brazil last week all the girls came up to me to touch me and it was heavenly. I didn't know my fan belt stretched that far. The girls gave me their phone #'s, addresses and pictures so I would know what was in store for me. Yep, they had nothing on except their hats; guess they didn't want to get over done by the sun. Ciao, Jimmy, the saxy thing from da Eu Es of Aye by way of Brooklyn and Queens.
Hot Chocolate—You Sexy Thing

Yes I know about freedom, it's more than just another word. Picture yourself in a state of being where you can't roam around as you would like to. Have you ever been in prison, all you get is a few hours in the court yard to feel the air and let it all hang out without bars, leg chains, or handcuffs? So don't tell me about freedom when you don't know what you got till you lose it or born in a dictatorship where you are told what, where, when & why. Me I would rather die than lose the most precious thing god gave us. Yes it's called freedom, never forget that for as long as you shall live . . .
Jimmy
Janis Joplin—Me And Bobby McGee

For your information I once had three 'You Tube' channels, dakotajim11378, my rock 'n roll channel, jimmyscomedyshop, just what it implies a comedy channel filled with all the funniest movies, commercials, standup comedians, and my prank stories. And last but not least the only one still active today, three, theloveman11378. It started out as a romance channel filled with the most romantic songs, movies, and poems to die for but I incorporated the other two channels into it, enjoy and please copy anything you like.

There's no charge but a tip is optional or at least send me a joke or two so I can share it with my friends, thanks Jimmy

Ps
I currently have over 370 playlists, so take anything that you want, I insist

Folks I got some good news but you better hold on tight because what I got to say will blow you and me away. I was talking to my fortune teller last night and that gypsy said her crystal ball told her I was going to meet a woman, possibly two but one was freaky. How freaky, one had thirteen toes, that's how freaky. Well now a day freaky is in and those are the kinds I like, don't ask. I'm going to party like there's no tomorrow. If you don't hear from me any time soon know I'm in good hands. How's that, two of them, one of me, you figure, need I draw you a picture, didn't think so, bye bye, so long, farewell, Jimmy, man on a mission, ménage a three
Lou Christie—The Gypsy Cried

Folks can you keep a secret, I dance for money, I know what you're all thinking, no way Jose, yes way I do, I do. It helps pay for the lifestyle that I'm so accustomed to. Only the best is what I get, and the best part it's all for free. My benefactors love me to death; they would do anything for this hahaha. Well this video is for you so what it's not your birthday, consider it an early birthday gift, yep for your birthday, ciao and how Jimmy, aka the Chippendale wanna be . . ,

Ps
Call me! I do house visits and even two, three, four girls at the same party
Chippendale—Happy Birthday

I'm thinking since I'm good with my hands, especially my fingers, don't ask, I could easily become a sculptor. My hands have been around some and I can put some clay together and make some statues, the naked kind what else is there. No, I don't need a model but then again that would be a bonus otherwise I would just close my eyes and presto it's done. They might even put it in some famous art museum next to Michel Angelo's. So if you're willing to be my naked Mona Lisa model send me your resume. I just know we're going to have a masterpiece and I will go down in history as the next Van Gough, or Shakespeare, or Pee Wee Herman, he's good with his hands too so I hear, ciao,
Jimmy, aka Jimmy Van Gough

My daddy once said never judge a book or a person by its cover or size, I can be ferocious as a lion and make love like a crocodile, yep like a beast when it's hot or is it in heat, same shit. I will rock your world and you will see stars galore. The last time I hooked up with a babe I think she's still in never never land, I bumped and thrusted with her all night long. She still has the shakes, my gyrations were too much, but now you know why they call me the love man. Call me, no I mean it, call me, I got something for you, and you, and especially you size nine. I will shake you, rattle you, and we'll be rolling in the hay all night long, bring it on, hahahahaha!!!
Bill Haley & His Comets—Shake, Rattle And Roll

Do you know what John Wayne, Clint Eastwood, and I have in common; we're all 'ass kickers.' Nobody in his or her right mind would ever f@#k with us cos we could be downright crazy and rip you apart starting with your eyes ball, your neck, or even your knee caps. See we are the heroes that this country needs so that any foe or so called friend would never take advantage or disrespect us. John, aka Big John, aka Duke, could punch your lights out. Clint, aka Dirty Harry would put a bullet in your eye balls with his eyes closed. Me, you don't want to know, let's just say they'll never find your remains once I'm finished with you. As my way of showing my respect to both Big John and Clint I'm going to play the lead in their biographies, who else could do the things I do and get away with it and be cheered, me, who else. See ya, hate to be ya, Jimmy

It's true what Rod Stewart says about some guys having all the luck, well I do and I think it has to do with the fact that I'm so cuddly and 'bubblicious.' Oh you don't think so, well one time with me and you will wish I was yours forever and ever. My therapist says I got it going on and she should know she was my wife not once, not twice, but three times so that proves I was a ham after all. Did I mention I'm a record holder but I'm not going to say why, all the girls I bedded know why but let's not talk about this here? It's my business and if you really want to know then you'll have to hook up with me and know I don't come cheap. I have class and everybody treats me with respect and showers me with lots of goodies. My fortune teller says I should be in the movies or on a stage, she thinks I would make for a good Chippendale, pack in the house wherever I go. She should know she's seen every bit of me and has a life size photo of me in her bedroom. She pretends we're lovers and when she goes to sleep and has one eye on me all night hahahaha. Guess I do have all the luck, I'm a hottie, ciao and how Jimmy
Rod Stewart—Some Guys Have All The Luck

When I started working at the tender age of ten, I would shine shoes and if I were lucky made a whopping five or ten dollars for the day. My pockets would be filled with lots of quarters, dimes, and nickels mostly tip monies. Well sometimes I would turn down a tip if a female client of mine offered to put on a show. What's a show; she would invite me over to her house as an excuse to shine all her shoes and in the process she would remove all her clothing right down to her hat. She just wanted to entertain me as I shined her shoes. Oh lordie lord that was worth my day's tips. I would offer it to her but she would just give me more money and the show she put on was for free and just for me. I think she had a thing for me. Oh how I miss them days, that's when I grew up to be a man hahaha, don't ask, byeeeeee, now where's that hat she gave me, I earned it, don't ask how!!!
Joe Cocker—You Can Leave Your Hat On

I got to ask you a question when do you know that you're a contender and it's time to kick it up a notch, let me explain. When you're dating, you know, going out with girls in hopes of finding Ms. Right and you think you've found a winner. Do you take the macho approach and grab her when you're escorting her home and when you're about to part does the man come out of you and you latch on to her like an octopus or do you gently take her hand and kiss it and off you go into the night. My buddies say I should be the aggressor, squeeze her good and tight and give her your all, whatever that means. But then I think it's her who has to make the first move, pull you into her bosom and rub your face all over

it. Oh well tonight I'll try another approach, pat her booty whenever she passes by and if she tends to pass by a lot than that's the sign you've been hoping for and you're in like flint, wish me luck. Tell you all about it some other day, well a man never tells, at least a gentleman that is, and that's me a gentleman through and through, and now a bona fide contender, ciao Jimmy
Marlon Brando—I Could Have Been A Contender

I got to come clean I think I have a wee bit touch of schizophrenia you know crazy like a fox in the cabeza, you know, in the head. It came about the time I was graduating from Long Island City High School and I went to the graduation ceremony in my birthday suit, well not in the open. I was just trying out my graduation attire, gown and hat, when I had completely forgotten I had not put on my trousers and shirt and when they called out my name there I was buck naked to the world in the rear and proud as a peacock because I was chosen the valedictorian or was it the school mascot, same shit, smart and goofy. Kindly do me a favor don't tell nobody about this because then I may have to come over there and kill you and feed you to the sharks, ciao and how, Jimmy
The End—Dom DeLuise

You've heard that expression, "nothing from nothing if you wanna be with me," is that the same thing as no tickie, no shirtie, oh than you've answered my question. It's like when I go into a strip club and if I don't tip the girls they don't dance up in front of my face, well I do know what it means now. When I go over to my girl's house tonight I'm going to tell her that, nothing for nothing if you wanna be with me and see what I get. Knowing her, everything and to top it off pudding pie a la mode, umm umm umm. I love me some a la mode, well got to go, got the urge for some nothing for nothing, ooooo weeee, bye bye, so long, farewell, Jimmy
Billy Preston—Nothing From Nothing

In one of my dreams I dreamt I was a king and my empire stretched from one continent to the next and by my side was the most charismatic beautiful woman I could ever want. She was worth her weight in gold, more valuable than 150 stallions or 150 camels and so damn smart and vivacious. All my time was spent just on her, making love like out of a story book novel. We begot two dozen kids and when not suckling my kids she would let me hahahaha told you it was a love story of immense proportions. Oh how I loved that woman so, she was my most treasured piece that diamonds and pearls could never replace or outshine. Ciao and how Jimmy, the king of the world
The Paradons—Diamonds And Pearls

My next book project is a love story of immense proportions. It's a story that will rock your world full of erotic dreams and desires and though the two individuals have innocently entered into a platonic relationship it will escalate into one of the greatest love stories ever imagined. Though they live thousands of miles apart their meeting was bound to happen. They are compatible in so many ways; they're talented writers, witty, and so compassionate. They end up writing to each other on a daily basis, not one day passes unless a family emergency kept them apart but then they come back and make up for it. Their story unfolds and it will rival any romance couple that ever lived. Their undying love and fantasies will

leave you in awe and will release all your inhibitions. By the time this book is over you too will be searching for that Mr. Right . . .
The Reflections—(Just Like) Romeo & Juliet

I'm currently doing some research on the subject of passion for the betterment of mankind, ok for me, and it's to determine if it's better to make love at night, in the morning, or in the afternoon. I guess it's all a matter of personal taste for each individual or as they say 'different strokes for different folks.' For some the best time for this coming together is during the afternoon cos that's when ones are at their best, well rested, well fed, and eager to release all the secret inhibitions bottled up inside. When you gaze into their eyes, or stroke them gently the sensations will be cataclysmic to no end. The scent of their mate's bodily fluids will be the aphrodisiac for one rocking good time lasting all day long with no end in sight. Read all about it in my next book, The Secret Inhibitions of a Woman, you won't find it on any book shelves; you'll have to beg me for it, hahahaha
Starland Vocal Band—Afternoon Delight

When I was a teenager my best friend got a job as a chauffeur and every now and then he would chauffeur me all over town, sometimes he would pick me up at school, what school, L.I.C.H,S. in NYC and the kids there especially the girls all wanted to be my friend. Yes, friends with benefits hahaha. I'd sometimes get a hundred one dollar bills and put a fifty dollar bill at each end and pretend I was a big spender hahaha. Now I know how Donald Trump feels, bet he's got wads of money in all his pockets, what did you think those bulges were, duh!!!

I was watching this infomercial on TV and this lady host shocked the heck out of me when she asked her audience how many people felt uncomfortable with their bras on, 95% of the ladies & 75% of the men raised their hands, there were only eight men. I say wear nothing and let it all hang out, go 'natural,' what say you!!!
Aretha Franklin—(You Make Me Feel Like) A Natural Woman (1967)

I was thinking about when I depart this here good earth how do I want to go out, in a casket or in an urn, and then it hit me, in a can of chock full of nuts, you know the heavenly coffee tin. I hear it's the best money can buy. Yep save my family the added expense of an expensive box, that I can't take with me no how, so that's my last request, maybe auction it off to the highest bidder. PT Barnum once said a sucker is born every minute, hahahaha I got a feeling they'll be one or two takers, hahahaha Jimmy
Blood, Sweat & Tears—And When I Die

Sometimes a person doesn't know his or her potentials till he samples every bit of what he hopes to aspire to be and so far I'm only half way there. I figure it's going to take me at least 30 to 40 years before I find out why I was put here in the first place, maybe to be a king, king of what I still don't know but when I find out you'll be the first to know, Jimmy has spoken!!!
Tony Orlando—Half Way To Paradise

I don't know if it was Captain Kirk or William Shakespeare who said "to be or not to be that is the question." Well, all I know if you **be** good to me, I'll **be** good to you, oh what a wonderful world this would be, good god, chicken on Sunday, hamburger on Monday, ooooo ooooo ooooo, Jimmy, the Ole English Actor . . . .

Hey, I never said I was a rocket scientist but I do recall telling you I was born at night but not last night. I can say when I wake up every morning it's you that I got on my mind so let the 'We Five' tell you some more, love you 'scooter pie' with all my heart and soul, umm umm umm
We Five—You Were On My Mind (1965)

Do you recall that movie Breakfast At Tiffany's, starring Audrey Hepburn and George Peppard well you know you've made it when you can have breakfast at Tiffany's and I'm going to go there soon and have my photo taken eating breakfast and I will become a celebrity and everybody will know my name. 'Jimmy at Tiffany's,' ooooooooo weeeeeeee every body's going to know my name!!!
Breakfast At Tiffany's • Moon River • Henry Mancini & Andy Williams

Folks did you know that the lowest form of slime on the face of the earth, are lawyers. They will take it all and here you thought they were out to protect you. Well I got news for you; all they got on their minds is where to get that next dollar. You see them chasing ambulances day in and day out, 24/7, and do you know why, cos that's money in their pockets, they can smell it a mile away. They have one rule, just follow the money. Well I'm going to be a lawyer someday. I watch all them lawyer shows. I've seen so many divorce court episodes I can be a divorce court lawyer in no time and it don't matter which side I'm on just as long as I get my fair share. I know how to be slick as some of those slicksters, they would have to get up before the rooster to pull a Willie over my eyes. Eyes like an eagle and sharp to the kill, that'll be me alrighty,
Jimmy ESP, LLC. INC. & CO.
Best of' Moments from 'Divorce Court'

Here's an oldie but goodie, ok so I've told it a few times before but not everybody's heard it so here it goes once more:
Confucius says man on street corner with hands in pockets, he aint crazy, just feeling little nuts . . .
hahahahahaha I thought you'd like it, it always cracks me up and when those folks in my work place hear the punch line they always pull their hands out of their pockets and that's even funnier. I just bust out laughing and they leave with a smile.
Ciao Jimmy

Folks in case you didn't already know I work part time in a home improvement store and when not selling my products or giving pointers I sneak in a joke or two. And that depends on what I see, if you're grumpy, then I tell you about my arm transplant or how I got in a scuffle with a lady bus driver because she called me a moron. I was at the end of the line minding my own business when it was my turn to get on the bus and she says "no moron," so I say what you mean no more on, I got to get on or I'll be late for work and

Mr. Ed won't take kindly to that. Oh you aint heard the best, how I'm always arguing with my mother-in-law or the time I won a gold fish after two hours of throwing quarters and finally bagged me one. You see I got no luck, when I won that jack pot in bingo so did 24 other folks so that 20 dollar prize we all got was just chump change. Oh well at least I got my sanity and my health, ciao Jimmy, hope to see you at the store, ask for Big Jim, you'll recognize me, I'm that handsome devil with the orange apron and a smile!

Folk music has always been one of my favorite genres and if you asked me to name my favorite folk group it would be this group. Dylan was a legend, The Byrds, superb, The Kingston Trio the best vocal harmony trio ever, but Peter, Paul, and Mary untouchable and they used their songs of protest to undo the wrongs of those who were evil and war mongers. Long live folk music and this awesome trio, thank you Jimmy!!!
Peter, Paul & Mary—If I Had A Hammer

Folks I got a tip I want to share with you that got me through in life and helped me be the man I am today. When you go on a job interview there are three things you should have on your person. One, clean shoes, two, a bow tie, and last but not least three, a pencil, and the more the better. You see I've gone to interviews and there all around me were some of the smartest people but they all lacked one of these three things that I mentioned above that would seal the job for them. These candidates had diplomas up the yang yang, and some even spoke two or three languages fluently which in today's world is a must. Me, I hate to brag I speak a half dozen languages, I speaka Spanish, Italiano, gutter talk, freaking Scottish or Irish, same shit, and parley vous Francais' so you know I know how to get over. The reason I always beat out those candidates is because I was the best equipped candidate and I always responded with yes sir or no mam so they could see I had etiquette. What am I doing today, I give motivational seminars and that's why all those folks come to my courses because they want to be like me, successful, a Mr. Big Stuff. Well hope to see you and please, please if nothing else bring a pencil wherever you go . . .
Jimmy
Jean Knight—Mr. Big Stuff

Enjoy this reply from a friend who added her own two cents of advice!!!

I always took spare underwear too just in case I got so nervous I pee'd myself. One time there were three men on the interview, they asked me some very hard questions firing them at me like bullets and I got a bit flustered and put my hand in my bag to get a hankie to wipe the sweat from my brow and gadzooks was it not my best pair of black and red lacy sexy panties. So I pretended nothing had happened, wiped my brow with them, blew my nose hard on them and put them back in my bag . . .

hahahahaha I saw them try to hide a little smile, it broke the ice and I got the job, but I'll be sure and take a pencil too next time

My reply back to her!!!! Wow I would never have thought of that, the red sexy lacy pantie trick, you sure knew how to lock in an interview. Bet them fellas were all over you hahahaha

Yesterday I saw a TV special about that guy George Willig, a twenty-eight year old part time toy inventor, who in May of 1977 scaled the South World Trade Center Building, all 110 floors by means of these window washer devices he had invented and made it to the very top in 3 1/2 hours. Two police officers in a window washer's bucket tried talking him down but he refused. He did manage to get to the top and was arrested and sent to the courthouse for arrangement where he was charged for reckless endangerment, criminal trespassing, and disorderly conduct. He was given I don't know how many hours of community service, yep cleaning windows. Well this gave me an idea so this morning I went over to my girl's house and climbed the telephone pole directly in front of her house to peep in to see what she was up to and she pretended not to see me and started to undress, took everything off, oooooo weeeee I nearly fell off the pole. I too was arrested and fined twenty five dollars and had to do twenty hours of community service pushing a broom all over town. Moral of the story, don't go tom peeping at your girl's house when you can look at her for free, well something like that, ciao Jimmy
George Willig—Scaling the WTC South Building

People ask me why am I so freaky, and I ask them in return, why do you say that. And they responded because you hang with some of the freakiest people. Hey, I don't tell you what to do with your fucking hair so don't go judging me. Ok so I talk about Mrs. Brown and my friend Mickey but it's all in jest. Heck, what else can I talk about, do you want me to tell you about the things your mama and I do, didn't think so. So please don't judge me, ciao, Jimmy

I've done everything under the sun and moon, climbed Mt. Kilimanjaro, Mt. Everest and gone to the bottom of the deep blue seas. Well to top that I'm going to write my memoirs. It will reveal a side of me you never knew existed because I can get weak at my knees for the one I love. When I'm finished you might even get to know her name because she's all that and a bag of ding dongs, ring dings, ho ho's, gummy bears, and scooter pies all rolled into one. Ciao got to start chapter one, don't wait up, Jimmy!!!
Elvis Costello—I Write The Book

When I hook up with a woman the first thing I look for is if she's got a diary. You see after dating her for a day or two I figure if I'm the man in her life I will see that in her writings. Last week she allowed me to move in guess my night cap rendezvous sealed the deal. So as she stepped outside to do some errands it gave me some time to search if she did have a diary. And right there in the top draw in her/our bedroom there it was a diary. So I opened it up and sure as I'm telling you this story she had written some very intimate romantic details of our relationship. I can't say what because what two consenting adults do in the bedroom, up against the walls, in the halls, on the floors, or on the roof is only for our ears and eyes. Let's just say I am the most with my manhandling. Well got to go we got plans for a hot bubble bath capped with a whole body massage, ciao, Jimmy
Little Anthony And The Imperials—The Diary

Girls can you kindly step aside for the moment because what I got to say is for the boys. Fellas just so you know there's never any trouble in my paradise cos I will kill for what is mine, so don't you even smile, wink, or utter a single word to my girl if you know what's

good for you. Oh, don't interpret that as being good for you but rather your demise is more like it and I hope your insurance premiums are up to date cos I will bury you. Oh you don't want to know what I'm capable of. Let's just say not a speck of your DNA will ever be found because the sharks and gators will devour you off the face of the earth and what you don't see I can't possibly be charged. Comprende, good, now be a good boy and let me talk to the ladies. Yes girls it's me again and this time I got something to say to you, call me if you should need a friend to get off your shoulders any problem that's bugging you, cos I can be more than just your handy man, good god!!!
The Crests—Trouble In Paradise

I got a true story I want to share with you. I believe in angels and that's the reason I'm still here on this good earth. I could have easily died a half dozen times and it's because those angels were/are watching down on me. And maybe they heard my prayers and rewarded me, allowing me to live another day and not go off into the deep end. Oh I do pray, it's nothing to be ashamed of cos any man worth his salt knows there is a god up above. Think about it, why are we here, somebody created this universe and put us here to do good. Oh there are also bad people but those are the ones you overcome with your goodness and sharing. I also believe in the afterlife and when it is my time I hope the doors will be open to let me in. Obviously we're not all going to get there cos our actions will dictate if and when we'll get there. In the meantime live your life helping your fellow man god rewards those who do just that. Enjoy this song it really says a lot, ciao Jimmy
Alabama—Angels Among Us

Folks I got some good news to tell you, with the holidays upon us again, I'm going to start my own hair cutting business. No I don't have a license nor do I need one. I'm experienced. I'll put a bowl over your head and clip away. What gave me the idea was when I was going through some old pictures and there we were, Mickey, Henry and me. What's that got to do with my hair cutting business? Back in the day when we were eleven or twelve Mickey and I gave Henry our first professional haircut, yep on Henrys noggin. We didn't do too good of a job but when you consider it was our first it was a masterpiece. Henry and Henry's father didn't think so but 'se la vie' is all I got to say and besides we saved Henry's father the two dollars it would cost to cut Henry's hair. Oh yeah we avoided walking past Henry's building in fear we might bump into Henry's father, he was a tough cookie, that was before Bruce Lee came around and from the stories we heard of Mr. King, that's Henry's father's name, that he would do karate on Henry and his siblings so we didn't take any chances. Well back to me, I can give you any style you want, the Mohawk look, the Kojak look, heck I can even put your initials at the back of your head, so if you're in town look me up. Jimmy's Barber Shop, where your dollar goes a long way. And for you ladies you're in luck I can give you a Brazilian waxing, you'll be looking sharp once I get through with you and there's no need to tip me, heck I might be tipping you, don't ask, hahahahaha bye bye, so long, farewell, Jimmy
High-top Fade | Sky Fade | Box Cut with Skin Fade

When I was a little bitty boy my sisters had to take me along if they wanted to go to the sock hops, you see my mother wanted me to chaperon those knuckleheads. Yeah they were my deepest nightmares, they watched American Bandstand every day after school hosted by

some dick head named Dick Clark and as a result I couldn't see Captain Kangaroo, Buster Crabbe, Jim Bowie, or Tarzan and all the cartoons, including Bozo, Mickey and Minnie, Daffy and Bugsy, and last but not least Popeye and Olive Oyl. So now they were going to pay if they wanted me to come along otherwise no deal. I requested a quarter from each one and I would buy me a pocketful of bubble gum. My pockets were filled to the brim. They danced every dance and I learned those steps and I would hop on to the dance floor and all the girls would line up to take a shot at me. All the older boys hated me because their girls wanted me, a cute little hunk who could dance up a storm. I learned everything, from the lindy, the stroll, the hucklebuck, Willie & the hand jive, the twist, the mashed potato, Mickey's Monkey, the jerk, the barefooting, the limbo rock, the bosa nova, the dog, the watusi, disco, and it didn't stop there, I can do all the modern ones too, popping, break dancing, the tango, el merengue, the mambo, the hokey pokey, the Macarena, and the list goes on and on. Who do you think gave the Evolution of Dance notoriety, yep me!!! Check it out, Jimmy
Evolution of Dance

I thought I had it bad check out this reply, well at least she could have it her way, enjoy, Jimmy

Wow what a nightmare indeed having to chaperone your sisters . . . I bet they weren't too happy about it either, bummer!!!
You missed your favorite programs, awwww I used to have to look after my little sister. Take her to dancing lessons, and singing lessons. She had two left feet and couldn't hold a note, and I had to sit outside and hear her caterwauling away. Ooohh gives me shivers up my spine just thinking about it. Then she took up Highland Dancing, which is dancing over crossed swords, let's just say that was the end of her dancing career when I sharpened those swords and she lost a couple of toes, ooops. Well accidents can happen, hahaha All I wanted to do was stay at home and watch Lassie, Old Yeller, Dick Van Dyke, Bewitched, Lost in Space, Shari Lewis and Lamb Chop. Noggin the Nog, Champion the Wonder Horse. hiiiiiiiiiiiii hooooooooo Silver . . .

And on a warm evening I would take her out in her wheelchair, and we'd go to the cinema where we booed and hissed and threw popcorn at the screen and tried to knock the usherette out with gobstoppers. and then later I'd park my sister on the brow of a hill and forget to put the handbrake on and she'd go careering down faster and faster laughing with glee, until she catapulted head over heels into the field of stinging nettles and crawled her way out and then we went home . . . yep . . . so many fond memories. hahahaha, Maggie

When I was head counselor at camp Lake Granada somewhere in Timbuktu or maybe it was Pottawattamie, I was put in charge of the medical department to treat all the kids who got sick or came down with any serious infections which included but not limited to poison ivy, cuts, and scratches, scurvy, insomnia, and so forth. I'm proud to report nobody died under my tenure. We had a few scares like the time my co-worker Sally Bender had to be resuscitated by me after nearly drowning but I came through like a trooper applied my hands to chest massaging and mouth to mouth and that was for almost a half hour in private hands on. So when I was on my way home to momma's house for some needed rest and relaxation they called out for somebody with medical background to assist in child birthing. This passenger was about to give birth so seeing nobody volunteered I raised my hand because I knew this was a dire emergency that required expertise tampering. Well not tampering but you get the idea hands on. So I yelled out get me some hot water, plenty of bandages, and a bottle of brandy, 100% proof. Why the brandy, I need courage to attempt this maneuver. I only assisted a handful of rabbits and chickens but that prepared me for what I needed to do.

Allan Sherman—Hello Mudduh, Hello Fadduh! (A Letter From Camp)

Now that I'm on the subject of grandmothers, mine was called 'Big Momma' and she was the ruler of the house, big daddy, aka grandfather didn't dare upset her no how because she was too much. Pardon the pun, she did weigh over 285 pounds and for a short lady of 5 feet 6 and a half that was big. Well any way I just wanted you to know she could be meaner than a junk yard dog. You heard of that 90s TV show 'Scared Straight' well it brought a bunch of convicts in prison to speak to those kids going down the path of crime and they would scare the living day lights of those juveniles who needed some scaring. If I had to choose one it would be Big Momma cos she would not hold back, would kick your ass in a split second. Those convicts could frighten you but were not allowed to touch you, not even a hair on their heads, but you didn't know that because god knows you dared to answer them back what might pursue. Check out my 'Scared Straight Playlist' but I must warn you there's a lot of cussing and it's meant to straighten out those delinquents. It sure scared me and I wasn't in those penitentiaries per say, and while you're at it enjoy the trailer, 'Big Momma's House' staring Martin Lawrence and at his best no less!!!

For those of you who aren't aware I'm a collector I go to flea markets every chance I get looking for some genuine artifacts that I can resell at a higher price and make a quick buck. Sometimes I come across a rare music album or a genie lamp. Well on Friday last as I was ready to leave I came across this naked female mannequin and it reminded me of the time when I was a kid of thirteen and I had an inflatable doll, I rather not talk about this but I can say my friends loved it. They would come over and pretend it was a real girl, dance with it, hold it, and all sorts of things. They would practice their dance moves in case one day they had the nerve to go to the Friday and Saturday Night Sock Hops and ask one of the girls to dance. My best friend who will remain anonymous borrowed it one night and when he brought it back a month later it had patches all over it and when I asked him why the holes he said his belt buckle popped it every time he took it for a whirl of a spin. I think he took it for more than a whirl like maybe slowed danced with it or some shit. What became of that doll, my mother caught my friend kissing it in the lips and hugging it to death she put a match to it. Hey let's not mention this ever again, people may get the wrong ideas. I was thinking I could dress up that mannequin for the holidays, like a snow woman, or the Easter Bunny or maybe just use it for target practice. I got me a pistola that I can use it on, you know what they say, practice makes perfect, and I'm drop dead perfect ask any girl, byeeeeeeee, Jimmy

Just For Laughs—Man Kisses Mannequin

Hey I don't know about you but I was raised old school, for those of you who don't understand when my parents or grandparents told us to do something it was done without lip or hesitation. With my dad or granddad it was one look and you knew to jump. My

grandmother was the enforcer, you stepped out of line one smack was all it took and it didn't matter where, at home, in school, or even at church. I look around today and I see kids out of control, spoiled, rotten and with filthy mouths. And those kids are prone to finish last in school, in jobs, and in life. What we need is a military style of professional people who can retrain those losers. It's obvious some of those kids had no proper upbringing but that's no reason to continue being a loser. When you reach the age of maturity 18, 21, or 25 then it's time for you to change your path in life and that should give you the encouragement to straighten up since it's now in your hands. For me it was a girl, yep I fell in love and she was the reason I now walk the line!!!
Johnny Cash—I Walk the Line

Folks I got to ask you a question, what do you do when you get unexpected visitors or visitors who don't know when it's time to go home. Oh this is one dilemma I can't resolve on my own so if you know how I should handle this situation please email me back with a suggestion. My daughter says I should in a nice way say "here's your hat, what's your hurry." Maybe I'll try that approach next time that somebody comes over and see if that works and when they finally get the hint put on this song and party. Ok, ok it's my mother-in-law who drives me to drink; she comes over at all hours of the day and wants to eat me out of house and home. She's one ugly good for nothing blood sucking creature from down under and I don't mean Australia, deeper than that, ciao, Jimmy and do enjoy the song!!!!
Ce Ce Peniston—Finally

Hey just kidding, I love that old lady to death and so do my kids but what do they know!!!!!

Check out these two replies!!!

I shout through the letter box `who goes there friend or foe` if they answer friend. I make them put their hand through the letter box, check out their fingerprints, and if it's someone I want I open the door and let them in. Now if they outstay their welcome, I go upstairs and put on my pj's and dressing gown, my wee Willie Winkie knitted bed hat, bed socks, and hot water bottle. and they generally get the hint. But if they say foe I get my cork gun out and blast it through the letterbox onto their groin area. And that usually does the trick I hear a few splutters and cusses and watch them go limping down the drive, hahaha it worked every time, ciao,
Maggie

I go upstairs take all my makeup off [and that's enough to make them run for the hills] and come back downstairs in my pj's, yawning hugging my teddy bear and a cup of cocoa, if they don't take the hint by then I say to them . . . Get Out My F . . . . g House, I'm Knackered And Need My Beauty Sleep!!!!!!!

Knackered, did she say what I think she said, oooooo weeee, I think she means business, hate to see her mad hahahahaha, Jimmy

Folks is it possible for two gay people, one a male and the other a female, to fall in love with each other. Well I'm writing an idea for a TV sitcom where this gay couple does just that, fall in love but then that changes everything around because they're no longer a gay couple but a heterosexual one. His name is Roberto and her name is Angelina, and they met at a wedding when they simultaneously saw the bride's 100% leather boots and they jointly asked her where she got them. At that new store in the Village called Simon's Haberdashery but they only had one left says the bride. So the very next day who do you think was in front of the store, yep Roberto and Angelina, it was seven AM and the store did not open till 9 so Roberto being the lady that he was invited Angelina for breakfast so they agreed and they talked till they couldn't no more. Now the only question was who was going to get that last pair of boots, so they decided to choose for it by playing rock, scissors, and paper. It was decided three out of five would be the winner. Roberto won and when they realized the time made their way to the store but then it was too late, it was 9:15 and somebody else had just snapped up that last pair. Roberto so heartbroken invites Angelina over to his crib for some leftover sushi and Angelina not able to resist sushi agreed and that's how this love story unfolds and the pilot of this made for TV program begins. They are almost the reincarnation of Lucy and Rickie and Ned and Stacy and inseparable from this point on. Now to sell it to the networks, and if it becomes a sitcom hope you all watch me at my best. Ok so I let the cat out of the box, yes I'm Roberto, but don't tell this to no one and what I do is my business and besides I'm a complete changed man since I met Angelina, ciao Jimmy

Nancy Sinatra—These Boots Are Made For Walking

Folks I got a story that will make you sick, well it has me sick already and I didn't even tell it to you yet. Talk about hanging on to your bloomers and toupees well this will blow them away. I was in an Irish pub with my Irish friend, Mickey J, the name has been changed to protect the innocent cos he's a wanted man somewhere, yeah that nutter who introduced me to a lot of crazy ideas. He was looking depressed so I asked him why the gloomy face. He told me he just heard an old flame of his had died. So I asked him how long ago, two weeks. So I jumped out of my seat after drinking that glass of tequila and we ran home to get two shovels and he wanted to know what for, so we can excavate her remains up. So he looks at me and says did you hear what I said, she's dead. Yeah but if you want to keep her alive we can taxidermy her body. What do you mean; she's deader than a door nail. So I sat him down and explained what I was planning to do if my lover girl dies. Stuff her up and mount her body on the wall like them game hunters do, but we're not just going to put her head up there, the whole body plus I can't bare cutting her head off that's too gruesome. So he asked me what I'm going to do with her body. So I smiled at him, when you freaking get that urge you mount her, you climb up a ladder and have your way with it. He smiled and gave me a great big ole hug that almost knocked the wind out of me. Now tell me I aint smart, brighter than a light bulb that's for sure. So we rush over to the graveyard and we dig her up. Well this is why I said hang on to your bloomers and toupees, her body was partially wormed up, you know decayed so I said oh well there goes your urges it's too late but if you want a souvenir that's all you can have. Hey you should see what I took, don't ask it's in my freezer next to the other chicken breasts. He took a piece of her heart. Now tell me I aint good for something, hey you got a love one I suggest you get them to sign a prenuptial agreement, that way you can satisfy your urges, byeeeee, Jimmy

Janis Joplin—Piece of My Heart

Aint that the truth, when I was doing time in the big house, all I could think about was that people got to be free. Every time I went out to the exercise yard I would envision me outside those damn barbed wires. Well I finally got out after twenty five long grueling years and I made a pledge to the parole board they were never going to see my stinking ugly face ever again. Before I spit on the ground or throw a cigarette bud on the floor I would have second thoughts cos I will never stoop so low to give them a reason to put me back in those chains, amen!!!
The Rascals—People Got To Be Free

Folks do you recall when I was writing my bucket to do list, well I got some good news I completed it last night, do you want to see what I've added to it since our last encounter, there are 3,011 things I want to do before I kick the bucket, that extra ten is for adults only. But I can tell you a few of them but you girls' better hold on to something cos what I got to say will blow you away, here goes:

I want to chase beaver in Hugh Hefner's mansion, yeah the two legged kind, I want to go skinny dipping with four of the most voluptuous women in all of Brazil. I want to go on a date with Pamela Anderson to some deserted island and all she does is feed me coconuts and popcorn. I can see me now jumping for joy and over stuffed till I'm completely satisfied ooooo weeeee. Yeah it's all naughty but nice escapades or should I say sexcapades hahahaha and you know I'll be more than rolling in the hay. We all got to go sometime and that sometime I hope it'll be me on the saddle, yahooo don't ask just wish me luck, bye bye, so long, sayonara, Jimmy
The Bucket List—Morgan Freeman & Jack Nicholson

Folks my Notebook Playlist is awesome, it has close to 75 videos in it at the present time and like my love, it's growing more and more each day. And for those of you not familiar with the movie I want to let you know that they die in each other's arms at the end. I know I spoiled it for you but that's the way I want to go. Not get hit by a car, drown in a lake, or get shot up. I want to die in my baby's arms, oooooo weeee. To be honest there's one better, yep while on the saddle. Good god in heaven that's far greater cos that means I was up and running and on top of the world, yes she is my world. Hey do you know a better way, didn't think so but tell me your choice, and no ménage à three thingy, thanks Jimmy

One of my favorite dicks of all time was this man you're looking at, the one with the squint eye and dirty ole raincoat, yes that's him Columbo aka Peter Falk. Man could he solve a homicide case like no other yet he couldn't get over on his wife. Napoleon had his Juliet or was it Josephine, Aristotle had his Jackie O and Columbo had Mrs. Columbo. Wow, what a pair bet she was the brains of the outfit cos that stumbling dick was a nerd if ever. Scotland Yard, the KGB, nor the Pink Panther wanted no part of him that's for sure, bye
Jimmy

Ps
Oh, one more thing, he set the bar for all the other private dicks to follow, end of story, period . . . .

Folks I think you already heard by now that my friend Felix made that death defying twenty four mile high jump from outer space well it was my idea and I had planned to do that historic jump first but somebody stole my parachute and he beat me to the punch. Well I'm going to do one better I'm going to go to our nearest planet, I think its Mercury, I know it starts with an M, no not Mars, it's definitely Mercury and jump from there to earth. I know it's going to take me a few weeks to get here maybe even longer but then I'm going to own that record and leave Felix in the dust so wish me luck and when I get back I expect a parade and lots of women at my doorstep. And yes, this is another one to bite the dust from my bucket list, damn I'm going to be bigger than Paul McCartney, Ellen DeGeneres, and Oprah Winfrey all put together. Yes that Oprah, have you ever heard of The Color Purple, yep that one, the one that smacked Harpo in the kisser, her. There's no end to my madness, see you when I get back, Jimmy, the space cadet and Guinness Record Holder again, don't ask!!!

For you folks new to my channel, I'm what is known as 'the great pretender,' and where better to pretend is at the store where I work in as a part time associate in the plumbing aisles. What's a great pretender thought you'd never ask. When I want to impress an old acquaintance or a hot chick I get into my great pretender persona. I simply put on my clip on bow tie and I yell out an order to one of my coworkers that the next time they come in late I'm going to have to let you go or I will pretend I'm on my IPhone giving orders to my chauffer to have my Rolls Royce ready in half an hour. Hahahaha I know that's crazy, my coworkers scratch their heads and they think to themselves he's a freaking maniac and that hot chick gives me a wink. Well it's things like this that got me ahead in the store especially in the plumbing department. I no longer have to push a broom or work the graveyard shift cos I'm also an 'ass kisser.' Whenever I see the boss coming I say how good he looks, I see you lost some weight, and I just love your shirt. Well he didn't lose a freaking thing, in fact he put some on, and that's the same old shirt he wears everyday but it does get me a smile and a big ole thank you. Get this, he invited me to his house for the holidays but I told him I couldn't make it cos I was dining with the Marquis of England and the next day going on a fox hunt with Sir William of Scotland. Well now you know how I suck up to people and why I'm the best at what I do, ciao, the Queen is calling me, wonder what she wants from me now, byeeeee, Sir Jimmy
The Platters—The Great Pretender

Folks you can add 'ass kisser' to my resume, yep I polish apples for my boss and that's not all I do for her. I'm the rat in the vessel at my workplace I tell her who's not working and who's doing who, and who took an extra break or stole a pen or some paper clips. I'm a one of a kind snitcher, best of the best and nothing gets past me. Well got to go here comes a shady co-worker going to keep an eye on her, byeeeeeeee, Jimmy
Hess Is More—Yes Boss

Love this reply below, enjoy!!!

Yikes!! you ass kissing apple polishing brown nosing backscratching kowtowing snitching boot licking sneaky fawning yes-man of the first degree. That resume is sure filling up, Maggie

Hahahahahahahahahahahahahahahaha, I just love that girl, as you can tell she's not in love with me, so who cares I got more women than I can shake a stick hahahahahahaha!!!
Jimmy

Yes that's what I like the most, sugar sugar, honey honey, and candy girls. Well not in that order, but I can say they're more than finger licking good. They call me their lollipop boy. Aint that the truth, they can't get enough of me and there's plenty of me to go around. So if you're looking for some excitement in your life, look me up, and we'll party till I can't get enough. Enjoy the song and remember my motto live, laugh and love . . .
Ciao, Jimmy
The Archies—Sugar Sugar

Folks I need to know is it true what they say about blondes having more fun, why I'm asking is because I'm thinking of dying my hair blonde. Guys like girls who are blondes; even though some aren't too smart but then smart aint important when you're having fun. I know, why me, the love man, well I'm just doing some research work in case I want to write another book and you know what my favorite topic is, women and what makes them tick. And in case you don't know I don't discriminate against anyone, you can be black, white, brown, red, or olive, and all kinds, big, small, rolly polly, those who got big backs, or no backs. Hey, as long as they aint got what I got, that's a keeper, must I draw you a picture.
Michael Jackson—Black Or White

Check out this reply from a fan, yes I do have fans, why you ask, you're jealous no doubt!!!

I don't think blondes have more fun particularly I have been all colors and I have had fun with blonde, brown, auburn, fire red, chestnut, get the picture hahahha

Yes I do, Leader of the Pack, hahahaha . . .

Folks I'm writing another book, this one is on the topic of women of the world. I haven't decided what to call it. Here are a few ideas I'm tossing around. 'What Women of the World Look For in a Man', or 'What Sensuous Women Want From a Sensuous Man,' Well in order for me to research the book I need to ask you a series of questions. Here is a sample of that questionnaire and if you can be so kind as to answer them for me and I promise I will keep it confidential.

1)   What turns you on about man?
2)   On a first date what will you allow him to do?
3)   Do you kiss on a first date?
4)   Will you let him take you home for a night cap?
5)   Do you know what a night cap is?
6)   Do you kiss and tell, you know, tell your friends what happens on your dates
7)   How do you like your man dressed, in a suit, sweat clothes, shorts, or with nothing on?
8)   Do you want him to kiss your cheek, hands, lips, neck, or where?
9)   When you dance, do you prefer the fast ones, like the mambo, tango etc, or the slow ones?

10) Do you prefer flowers, candy, or jewelry as a gift?
11) Do you like sushi?
12) What do you have on when you go to sleep?
13) Do you like breakfast in bed or on the floor?
14) What is your favorite romantic movie?
15) What is your fantasy about men?
16) Do you allow your man to remove the ribbon from your hair, why, or why not?

Well this is just part of my research work that I will need to know, then maybe I might come over to meet you face to face to get up close and personal to really get to know the true you and ask you some more questions. What's in it for you, me. Who knows we can become the best of friends and what that can lead to next. Ciao got to go, need to choose a book cover and the book title, maybe you got a title to recommend, it might be the one I choose and I'll let my readers know who gave me the idea . . .
John Lennon—Woman

Check out these responses from three dear friends, enjoy Jimmy

Re: theloveman11378 sent you a video: "John Lennon—Woman HD

1) His lips and fingers
2) Probe me all he wants
3) Can't stop kissing him from head to toe and then some
4) That's a must. His or mine I don't care just put that do not disturb sign that we went fishing
5) Sure when the fish are jumping or is it biting, same thing
6) Only my therapist and he wants the whole 9 yards and then I charge
7) Nothing on, that's a no brainer
8) Everywhere and I mean everywhere both my lips too
9) The slow dirty dancing ones to get my juices flowing nonstop
10) Just him
11) Love it, I just devour it to pieces lick it good and fast
12) Nada freaking thing on except some soft romantic music to set my night on fire
13) Anywhere I can chew it up
14) The English Patient remake
15) I fantasize about just one man, he's a hunk, irresistibly delicious and his name is, the love man
16) That hunk can remove anything he wants, his clothes and mine is really how I prefer it cos I don't want to waste any time if you get my drift

Re: theloveman11378 sent you a video: "John Lennon—Woman HD
"✿(̄•., ♥♥ ,.•´ ̄)✿
lolololol . . . . those answers above were your OWN funny answers to your own questions,. you get madder & madder!
Well here's mine below

1) Good physique
2) Polish my shoes
3) Oh no, no, no
4) Oh no, no, no
5) Hot chocolate, durgh . . . . you silly billy!
6) No, they too nosey
7) Chinos & shirt with Gucci shoes
8) Cheek
9) A Salsa
10) Jewelry
11) Yes . . . . like billhe
12) MADEMOISELLE
13) On the table
14) Mary Poppins
15) That would be telling
16) Not . . . . because my hair is too short

. . . have you a 4ft Japanese dwarf lined up?
Pleasant dreams, L
Re:theloveman11378 sent you a video: "John Lennon—Woman HD"

1) Hahahahahahahahahahahahahahahahahahahaha
2) Hahahahahahahahahahahahahahahahahahahaha
3) Hahahahahahahahahahahahahahahahahahahaha
4) As if I`m gonna answer any of your questions
5) Hahahahahahahahahahahahahahahahahahahaha
6) Hahahahahahahahahahahahahahahahahahahaha
7) Hahahahahahahahahahahahahahahahahahahaha
8) No cotton picking way Jose
9) Nada
10) Hahahahahahahahahahahahahahahahahahahaha
11) Nice try Mr. Correa
12) Hahahahahahahahahahahahahahahahahahahaha
13) Gotta hand it to you, you`re cute
14) hahahahahahahahahahahahahahahahahahahaha
15) Confidential!! hahahahahahahahahahahahahaha
16) 10 out of 10 for trying hahahahahahahahahahaha

And I wish you luck with your research :))
M

I hope you like this video. It's the real me that I just had to show you, well not exactly me, I'm a hunk and obnoxious in a good way. Put it this way if we went out on a date I would have you crying from laughing so hard, you would have stomach pains and you might even pee on yourself, then that's when we would have to part as friends cos I don't know you and you would have to deal with the restaurant owner as who will be cleaning up that mess on the floor. Bye bye and please don't do anything I wouldn't do, enjoy, Jimmy

Ps
I spent ten years in a mental institution I was only supposed to be in there ten weeks it turned out to be the best years of my life.
The End—Dom DeLuise

Love this reply below!!!

hahahaha . . . yep I remember those ten weeks er years. Who cares time flies when you're a loony tune . . . but what fun we had. Remember the time we found the closet where the doctor and nurses kept their uniforms, and we dressed up, and you went round the wards taking everyone's temperature in a place where the sun don't shine and I dished out the happy pills hahahahahaha and then we all escaped outa that place, and did the conga into the garden, through the gates, over the barbed wire fence and down the road . . . their white gowns flapping in the breeze, as we laughed and joked. You examining my chest as I played with your stethoscope, ahhhh memories . . . memories . . .
Shame the cops caught us as we were on the second verse of hokey pokey, but thems the breaks. hahaha
M.

Guys always ask me why am I so successful with the ladies, what is it that I do, well I hate giving away my trade secrets but I do know the art of seduction. First, you got to set the trap, well not really a trap just get the right atmosphere in motion to make that lady putty in your arms. A romantic dinner for two with scented candles is a must, a good bottle of booze to get her at ease to open her up. Then you put on some soft romantic music, a little Freddie Jackson, some Al Green, Michael Bolton, The Delfonics, Smokey, Teddy and last but not least some Barry White. By this time she should be ripe for the taking. Get her on the dance floor, lay down some of your best sweet talking lingo and whisper a few sweet nothings in her ears to drive her up the wall and bingo she's all yours. You top it with a choice of a hot steamy bubble bath or a massage to kill for with some ying yang massage oil. Be the gentleman that you are and let her choose her poison and she'll respect you for that. It always works for me.
Good luck Jimmy

Ps
Don't forget to put up that 'do not disturb gone fishing' sign hahahaha

I got some good news, I applied for a job at the NYPD, and as part of their security investigation they go through everything in your life history. But how am I supposed to remember everything that I did. And why my grade school activities. I was young and naïve, hung with the wrong kind of girls, and why bring it up. Why not talk about what I did when I was 21 not 8 or 9. I got this funny feeling Ms. Rachett, my 3rd grade teacher is behind this, she can't forgive me for when I gave her a beaten in class. So wish me luck and say a prayer for me, I've been practicing my gun duel tactics with Pookie, I chase her all

around the house. Poor cat, got so much paint on her she looks more like a calico instead of an orange tabby. Don't tell this to anyone cos animal control will report me and there goes my job, yep to be one of NY's finest. Bye bye I see a suspect lurking outside got to get my zap gun and my night stick to do some surveillance.
Jimmy, aka Officer Jimmy
The Earls—Remember Then

Hey if I get that job, as NY's Finest in the NYPD, I will kick ass, cos there's going to be a new Marshall in town and all those dirt bags, dope dealers, and you know who you are will get my wrath. I will put a hurting on you, you will think you just met your maker and you'll end up on the chain gang for sure. So you better walk that straight line from here on now, Jimmy, aka Marshall Jim

My therapist thinks cos I love making pottery I got a feminine side about me, well she don't know the whole story. I invite girls over so I can teach them how to make pottery but the real reason is so I can seduce them. See as I sit behind them I get to feel them all over and that's my way of teasing them and that leads to a little mud wrestling and a skip and a hop to my bed. I got the idea from watching this movie 'Ghost' starring Patrick Swayze and Demi Moore. I got a basement full of pottery, one day going to throw a pottery going out of business sale, you need any ash trays, cups, I got 'em. You want to learn how to make pottery, I'm your man, just book an appointment, yeah I got lots of women who want me, I mean who want me to teach them the how to of pottery. You will just love me, ciao, Jimmy, the Girlie Man
The Righteous Brothers—Unchained Melody (Ghost)

. . . yes I'm a rebel, been one since grade school. Did I tell you the time I stole a motorcycle when I was ten and that should have been a red flag that I wasn't going to be any good. Well it didn't stop there, the taxi, the bus, and that tractor trailer, there was nothing I couldn't hot wire. That train hijack was not me but I was blamed for that too just the same, did five years in the pokey, don't remind me. I also had a good side, girls were crazy for me, guess they liked that mean streak in me. I broke many a heart in the process, see I couldn't stay put, anywhere I went girls wanted the kid and as a gentleman I always obliged them. You know made love to them. That red head in the Chevrolet was da bomb; she had me begging her for more and more. Well I was no good still am no good, don't let your daughters or wives come near me, I will steal them and use them and who knows what this bad ass can do, ciao, Jimmy, the rebel
The Crystals—He's A Rebel (1963)

Hey you recall how I became a misfit getting into all kinds of trouble, like the time Mickey and I gave poor old Henry a haircut leaving him with tons of bald spots and no sideburns and we were just twelve or thirteen. And that time I was sent to reformatory school for six months cos I beat up on my third grade teacher Ms. Rachett. Well she didn't have to bite, kick, and pull my hair. I just did it back but with lots of force and gusto. Like it says in the good book, an eye for an eye, a tooth for a tooth that's what I gave her. I got some more to tell you, whenever we had a sleep over at my house I would invite two or three friends on the weekend and what we did to one of the kids is a crying shame. We would go off to sleep

at midnight after looking at a bunch of girlie magazines and I'd wake up one of the guys and we would do some crazy shit. Paint the other guy's toe nails while still sleeping, yellow or pink or black. Then with my sister's eye brow pencil and mascara performed some heavy duty makeover. Eye brows twice the size and a lip stick touch up and presto he looked like a hot child from the city. The next morning we would get up bright and early and wake him up. When he saw us laughing didn't know why till he looked into the mirror and almost had a heart attack. He quickly jumped into the tub and took a long hot shower and was able to remove most of it except he looked like he had two black eyes and his toe nails, well nothing he did would remove that black paint. So I told him when he gets home take some turpentine and that should do the trick. He would never do another sleepover ever again, we call him Roxanne. Hey, here's the clincher we took some glossy photos and we blackmail him for some money every now and then. I know I was wicked but then that's why I always ended up in reformatory school or in jail. Hey don't do any sleepovers at my house cos you will never live it down. Ciao, Jimmy
Nick Gilder—Hot Child In The City

Folks I got an embarrassing story to reveal, I love food and certain foods have a bad effect on me and probably most other people as well. My best friend Joeseppie used to invite me over to his house to eat Italian food; you guessed it they were of Italian heritage. His mother and sisters, all six of them, would cook up a storm of pasta fazool. What is pasta fazool, pasta with beans, and you know what beans can do to you, yep the more you eat the more you fart, pardon the phrase but it's true. Why did I go there, well besides a free meal, to see his sisters, they were hot to trot, so it was on their account that I even heard of pasta fazool. Angelina, Rosita, Maria, Lucia, Sofia and Rosalina were their names and I loved them all. I went out with them, no, not all at the same time separately, omg they made love like they made pasta fazool, incredibly delicious. I know it's true how beans are a healthy food but awful in the after affects. We had to keep the windows wide open as we made love but then the neighbors would be peeping in. But who cares when you're having a good time, it was love at first fart, I mean at first sight, bye bye Jimmy
Dean Martin—That's Amore

Folks you've heard the expression 'my boat has come in,' well it's come in big time. How's that you ask, Oprah's having my baby so you know I've hit it big. Who's Oprah, why no other than Miss Harpo, Oprah Winfrey. Yeah we met when I was a guest on her show. I was all dressed up with nowhere to go and she spotted me in the crowd. I was wearing my new spandex hot pink outfit and my pink go-go boots and that was all she had to see. She invited me over to her house for a night cap and I showed her my all and she showed me her all and before you knew it we made love the whole night through. Hey don't tell nobody cos it will get into the tabloids and then Stedman will find out and it may kill him so we want to break it to him gently. I won't ever have to work another day in my life again except pamper that woman to death. Well I hope you're all excited for me and maybe I'll invite you all to my wedding. When's that, when I hook it up, Oprah's got a way about her so when I wrap her around my fingers some more then maybe I pop the question. She's going to love the kid and I will take her to heaven and the moon, heck anywhere she wants to go, she's got limos, boats, planes, and now me. Hey her boat's come in too hahahaha. Byeeeeeeeee
Jimmy, Mr. Harpo

Juice Newton:—Break It To Me Gently

I've told you many things about me but not everything so I'm going to tell you something I've never told anybody, I'm an eccentric S.O.B. How's that, good question, when I walk outside I don't step on cracks, I run indoors when I see or hear a bus or a truck coming cos I'm afraid of the noise and the pollution they omit. When a plane or a helicopter passes over head I also run in, I think they're going to crash down on me. And if that's not enough I'm even afraid of my own shadow, I think it's following me and out to choke me. My therapist says I'm nuts and I guess she's right but I'm alive and that's all that matters. A person can't be too careful now a day. Hey, that's not all when I hear a fire truck, a police car with its sirens on, I'm crouching underneath the nearest car cos that too scares the hell out of me. I'm thinking of moving to some deserted part of town. Oh boy, here comes an ambulance and you know what that means, hey didn't you read the words that were coming out of my fingertips, get on the ball you freaking morons . . . .
Jimmy, aka Mr. Eccentric
Baby Scared of Her Own Shadow

Here's another story I've never told anybody before, I've been with my girl now for over two years, six months, and 21 days but who's counting. Well she's everything a man could possibly want; gorgeous, witty, caring and sweeter than a honey bee, but she's got one flaw. Now I know you've heard of folks being born with an extra finger or toe well honey bunch got 13 toes and she wears clod hoppers to hide it from the public. But here's the best part when we get to making love she wraps her feet around me and that girl can go. Need I explain or draw you a picture. That woman makes love to die for. Yep it's the extra toes that give her that extra giddy up. So I got to say I'm blessed. Ok so the clod hoppers aint too pretty but I would never change a thing about her, toes and all. Hey keep this to yourself, what we do is our own business and don't be spreading this out, c ya. Jimmy
The Four Tops—I Can't Help Myself (Sugar Pie, Honey Bunch)

I don't recall if I ever told you that I got three older sisters, yep I was the baby in the family and whenever I wanted to watch some of my favorite shows on TV they would overpower me and put on American Bandstand. I wanted to watch Captain Kangaroo, Hop-A-Long Cassidy, Buster Crabbe, or Popeye but they always had to have it their way. They would dance along with the kids on TV and that got me even madder. Ooh I hated that guy who would shake his hips I think his name was Mavis or Pelvis or some shit. Well it was because of my sisters I hated girls in my pre-teen years, don't remind me. So how was it in your early years, did you have the same problems, tell me all about it, ciao Jimmy
Elvis—Hound Dog

Hey here's another of my many talents, as most of you already know I'm a bag of chips and it's because I know how to please the womenfolk that I'm so exceptional. I know what you're thinking, what is it that I do that drives the womenfolk crazy. Ok I'll tell you, I know what women want, they want a man that will please them, and tease them, and most of all excite them to no end. Well that's what I do, for instance if a woman has just been dumped I get them back on track, I remind them that there's too many fish in the sea so as not to give up on life, to get back on the horse, pardon the pun and get yourself a real barracuda.

And I tell them life is a bowl of cherries so try out some new flavors, and last but not least I whisper sweet nothings into their ear and bingo I hit jackpot. They then want to follow me everywhere. Ciao Jimmy aka the love man!
Brenda Lee—Sweet Nothin's

Here's another story that will put shivers up your spine, you all know I was incarcerated a bunch of other times. Well my therapist narrowed it down as to why I was no good. You see when I was in grammar school, at the age of nine or ten, I was the class clown, always said something funny or obnoxious and the teachers couldn't stand me and if they could, would have chipped in to put out a hit contract on my ass. Now it was customary whenever a student misbehaved that they put him or her standing at the back corner of the room as punishment well in my case I was always speaking out of turn but they didn't realize I was trying to reach out for help but it all boiled down to was that I could have been a somebody, a motivational speaker, or a CEO of Apple or Dunkin-Donuts or some shit. So any way while I was standing at the corner of the room I would always disrupt the class one way or another. I mean I couldn't help it if I farted, heck I'm human and so was Miss Rachett but why she would yell at me was just too much. I had to set her straight so I yelled back and then we got to shoving, and biting, and kicking and that's when I was kicked out of school and ended up in a reformatory school. So yes that was the straw that broke the camel's back. Look at me today; I'm one mean low down mother tucker you don't want to tangle with cos I will kick your ass to a pulp. Moral of story, don't freaking mess with Jimmy Correa and you can still buy my You Tube prank story book at any local Barnes & Noble or at my publisher iUniverse.com. Ciao and how, Jimmy . . .
Linda Ronstadt—You're No Good

Here's a reply from a friend, I think she's trying to tell me something.

hahahahahaha you can`t fool us . . . you low down mother tucker kick ass to pulp, reformatory, farting low down never do well . . . We know it's all cock and bull and you`re nothing more than a big softy. hahaha ciao Maggie

Recently I put an ad in the newspaper hoping to meet hot sexy girls. I wrote, sexy hunk, that's me, looking for a gal to paint my toe nails, then I paint her toe nails, then we paint up the town red and to drink piña coladas till the cows come home. Guess what, I got over 500 responders, now I'm sick of piña coladas and so exhausted I'm too pooped to pop. Need to find a resting home for the weary and all dried out, don't ask, ciao Jimmy
Rupert Holmes—Escape (The Piña Colada Song)

A couple of months ago I told you about my pole dancing competition, well while I was up in the air everything that shouldn't have popped out popped out and I was not only the laughing stock of the entire competition but I was also a big hit with a lot of the girls. You see they liked what they saw and as I was leaving the building I noticed a lot of them were following me home. All I know I get lots of fan mail each and every day and many send me photos of themselves in their birthday suits. I guess they figured they saw me in mine and one good turn deserves another. Oh well when they got it like I got it they like to flaunt it and flaunt it they sure did, hahahaha. Enjoy Peggy March she too was one of them there girls who followed me home, Byeeeeee, Jimmy

Peggy March—I Will Follow Him

Folks I got me a woman that is out of this world, she's everything a man could possibly want and then some. Let me explain, I was at the tomato counter picking tomatoes when I bumped into her. So I asked her if she could help me choose some good ones and she smiled and then that's when I knew I had to make her mine. I invited her up to my place for a night cap and the rest is history. She makes love like a Mona Lisa, she's my diamond in the rough, and I just polish her up and it's heaven all night long. Well got to go we're giving each other a massage and then taking a dip in the hot tub, don't wait around this will take all night, ciao Jimmy
Nat King Cole—Mona Lisa

Recently I heard this phrase "Je Ne Sais Quoi" can somebody out there in You Tube or Facebook kindly tell me what it means. It sounds sexy and something I would say to a lady if we were making love, so please interpret it for me. I think it means something in Greek but what do I know. Everything is Greek to me, other than 'opa' and 'ouzo.' Thanks. Jimmy

See the two responses I got back concerning 'Je Ne Sais Quoi,' glad somebody was listening!

This is my interpretation of 'Je Ne Sais Quoi,' that lovely warm feeling deep inside that wets your whistle and makes life so wonderful. That desire for another that you can smell, taste, and feel. It's what makes hearts beat faster, and arouses the senses to be one with another, ohhhhh . . . it's making long sweet hot passionate love together . . . . giving it all up to another . . . Lying in each other's arms, and sharing hot sensual desires and fulfilling sexual fantasies . . .

It means she has a certain something about her, a special quality. xoxo
Je Ne Sais Quoi (Mysterious Quality—an indefinable quality that makes somebody or something more attractive or interesting

Yesiree I couldn't have said it any better myself, these replies above do refer to me to a 'T'!

Somebody once asked me, what is it that you want that you never had or did. Well besides getting my picture on the cover of the Rolling Stone I wish I had a harem of girls like Hugh Hefner has in his mansion or those rich sheiks with all those camels and belly dancers. You see I want to be rich and famous, and have groupies knocking down my door wanting to party till I can't get enough. But I'm not going to hold my breath, you got to earn them perks and groupies so when my books start to sell then maybe I can hook up with the babes and party till I drop or can't find the door out hahaha. Well I'm going to put out an advertisement "Wealthy hunk, ok so I'm not wealthy but a hunk first class I am, thank you, looking for girls seeking adventure, travel and the good life. Send your credentials and photos to the address listed at the bottom, thank you Jimmy, The Master
Dr. Hook And The Medicine Show—Cover of The Rolling Stone

Folks I got some good news to report, I'm going to be rich and famous and get this, are you ready, you better hold on to something, star in a movie, and all I got to do is sing like

a cowboy. Heck that's a mighty tall order considering I can't even ride a horse but sing, choo anybody can sing, doesn't mean I'm going to be good at it but I'll be rehearsing this Josh Turner song and I got two days before I go in and do my scene. Here check this out, "BABY LOCK THE DOOR AND TURN THE LIGHTS DOWN LOW," yep that was me singing and later today going to buy me some spurs and a cowboy hat they call them a Stetson. I'm also going to do my John Wayne walk cos I got to look macho and authentic. Tell you some more some other time, got to go rehearse and rehearse, bye bye, Jimmy
Josh Turner—Your Man

Hey I'm no singer, heck I can't sing a lick to save my life but if there's one song that I wish I could sing to my woman this would be the one cos it says everything I want to say to that girl of mine. She shall remain anonymous cos I don't want anybody stealing her away from me, I would surely die without her. She's the best thing since the invention of the airplane cos I get high just thinking of her, love you girl, Jimmy
Keith Urban—Making Memories Of Us

I got a story that will knock your socks off. I was at a local topless bar the other day when this motorcycle guy walks in and has the nerve to tell me what the f@#% I was looking at. So I told him don't mind me, I was in the war and while in one of my drinking binges I got so drunk they say I screwed a parrot. I thought maybe you might have been one of my offsprings. I mean he was tore up from the floor up, earrings in his ears, nose, face and cocky as hell. So then I took a handful of his throat and he got down and begged daddy, that's me, for mercy, end of story, period . . . .
Jimmy

Folks I got a story but it's more of a confession, I have a therapist and I can't do anything without her guidance or advice. You see I'm afraid of everything, my shadow, a full moon, tall buildings, elevators, talking dogs, swimming by myself, and even showering alone. When I walk down the street I avoid stepping onto cracks, motorcycles scare me to death, and a group of anything is the worst, I envision them, it, snatching me and eating me up alive. So please don't divulge this to anyone cos I might have to kill you, you don't want to know. Have I killed anyone, sure, at last count seven but that therapist gives me a note every time I go to court and the judge lets me off for time served. How much time have I served, five years, but I must admit the best 15 years of my life. I hooked up with a bunch of nuts and they cured me cos I knew I had to get out of there cos they were crazier than me. I met Jack Nicholson; you know "One Flew Over The Cuckoo's Nest" Jack Nicholson, and Moms Mabley, the axe murderer, and Tuitti Fruitti. Who's Tuitti Frutti, the fruitiest serial killer of them all. She would ask you up for a night cap and would poison you up after having her way with you. So you see my therapist is the coolest and sexiest porn star that ever lived, well she has to make a living somehow, therapy isn't the only thing she gives, don't ask.
Ciao, I'm off to see the wizard, Jimmy
What About Bob—Richard Dreyfuss and Bill Murray

I've been getting a lot of invitations to those dating sites through the internet, why last week I got 'Meet Jewish Girls,' 'Arabian Girls', 'Russian Girls', 'Hot Latinas', 'Scrumptious Irish Girls', Irresistible Italian Girls', Sexy Scottish Babes. I paid a visit to my fortune teller and without me saying a word she said I was going to meet a whole slew of women and the only way that is going to happen is if I join those web sites, what do I got to lose. I was wondering if anybody in YT has gone through this experience. They ask personal questions like am I interested in easy girls, or them hard to get ones. What a dumb question, easy ones of course. Then they ask if sex is my priority or just meeting intellectual sophisticated women. I don't know where they get these questions any moron would know the answer to that, sex. Can't get none that's why I'm here to get more than I can chew, hahahaha pardon the pun. Then they want to know nationality, color skin, color hair, color eyes, tall or short, if measurement a key factor. Good god, the only thing important to me is that they don't have what I got, or blind, or in a wheel chair otherwise any ole woman will do. Beggars can't be choosey but I do want something to grab on to when we get down. You ever see them movies where they are ripping off each other's clothes, well that's what I seek, one hot feisty woman' to knock my socks off, make me scream and holler and bend for her. Let me put it another way, I'm a hunk, just dying to climb Mt. Everest and she has to be easy, fun loving, and willing to venture to the unknown, take me to heights I've never been too, and show me what she has from top to bottom If you know anybody like that send her my way. I will devour her, bye bye, Jimmy, aka the love man . . . .

The Brooklyn Bridge—Worst That Could Happen

I was talking to my therapist and that woman told me I should reinvent myself, now that's a problem cos when I look around they already have invented everything man can possibly want, ok ok and women. I mean the wheel has been here since the time of the modern caveman and pockets on T-shirts god knows when so what is it that I can invent. Hey if you know the answer to that let me know we'll go 50 50, no really, you get 50 and I get 50 cos I'm as honest as the day is long. C ya, going back to bed and dream of something, anything to make me rich!!!!

I got it, I got it, when you go to the beach what is it that you see on men, let me put it another way, have you noticed how men are getting top heavy, so why not invent a man bra or a one piece bathing suit for men the way they do for women. I mean a bosom on a lady is phenomenal but on a man uurrgggghh disgusting so that will be my contribution, one giant leap for man, one giant leap for mankind, hahahahaha . . . .

Jimmy, the haberdasher

People ask me is there any particular place where to hook up with the opposite sex. Yes siree Bob, I know a place, anywhere there are people. I like to find my women at a local library, at a fruit stand, in a museum, at a coffee shop; in a movie theater especially during those romantic ones when girls come alone and if you're lucky and play your cards right you might get to take her home. Me, I shuffle right into a chair next to one and within time, a minute or two later, I offer her some popcorn, a slug of booze from my pocket gold decanter and if I'm lucky she gets drunk or horny or both and presto she'll be calling me daddy and to the nearest park bench we go hahaha. Also last but not least in a bar. Now in a bar you got to be extra careful cos once you start to drink the dog inside of you comes out. What do I mean, you're getting a buzz and at this point in time anything on two legs looks good even the horny ones look good for the taking hahaha and before you know it it's a para bing, para bang, thank you mam. Well I got to go wet my whistle, we're due for an encore, ciao Jimmy

The Staple Singers—I'll Take You There

Folks I got a problem that not even my therapist or fortune teller can give me some sound advice to set me straight. I'm putting my laundry out there hoping somebody can get me out of this rut I'm in. As you all know I got it going on, my resume speaks for itself but I need to reinvent myself. My publisher says to think out of the box, goodness gracious I'm always in the box, my women say I should slow down my horses I can't help if I'm a hunk always waiting to happen so I'm going to have to push the envelope and come out of the closet with some new ideas. Hey if you got any ideas send me your suggestions. Ciao and how Jimmy

Diana Ross—I'm Coming Out

It is said that literature is the imitation of life. I don't know about you but my life has had its fair share of ups and downs and without a doubt love has been the focal point of it all. Have you ever been in a love relationship and not just for the lust but beyond that? The definition of love is the bond between two people and all the good things that come out of it. For me it's a feeling that makes me do summersaults whenever I think of her. I close my eyes and I see her, she's everything to me. She brings out the man in me. I just want to spend my life with her, hold her and squeeze her, walk along side of her. The letters that I have written to her would be the stuff romantic books, movies, and poems are based on. Words that songwriters would die for to be used in their lyrics that could easily melt you away. So yes it's true literature has had a helping hand in the making of some of the greatest stories ever written. Well maybe I should become a novelist or a poet or even a songwriter cos I've been through it all and who knows I'll be the next William Shakespeare or Al Jolson. Ciao I feel a sonnet coming on, Mammy, how I love ya . . . . Jimmy

I don't know if I ever told you this but Clint Eastwood got his start from me, you see I played the original Dirty Harry on Broadway and I was one bad dude. I would make anybody's day with what I had. You don't believe me well you don't want me to blow your brains out do you punk cos I will kill you without a blink. And those spaghetti westerns were also my doing, I would go over to that country the one that has the shape of a boot, no not Australia that one is down under but no shape or form of a boot. I think it's called Sicily or Malta and we made a whole slew of them westerns, that's how I met Mama Leoni, omg you should see her, all that and a bag of pasta, hahahahaha. I could devour her up in no time, don't ask. In fact I wrote all those western scripts, "The Good, The Bad, and The Ugly," "Hang 'em High." and "A Fistful of Dollars." Well I got to go, Clint's on the phone, ciao, Jimmy

Ps

Enjoy 'Play Misty For Me,' I taught him all he knows including how to manhandle a woman

Hey folks do you know what Fred Sanford and I got in common, not a freaking thing except we are business savvy in so many ways. He knows how to make a buck the illegal way, me the honest way. I'm going to throw a yard sale of the yard sales event every week this month. I'll post a 'going out of business' sign, and that's when folks by the droves come over expecting to find some good stuff. Remember someone's junk is another one's treasure. I got some old used underwear why chuck 'em when I can find a sucker to buy them for a nickel each, that's a nickel in my pocket and an old fruit of the loom, one of a kind underwear for some cheap so and so. Yes, one hand washes the other, well if you're smart come on over. They say the early worm catches the bird or something like that but you get my drift. You got to be there to score big at my yard sales. I got an old trench coat I found in Columbo's trash can; now tell me you wouldn't want to own it. Hey Columbo had his use for it just not useful any more to him but it would surely look good on you. So hurry over I got many other one of a kind deals. I got an old Elvis scarf and one of his shoes. Why one, cos I donated the other one to the Smithsonian Institute for the blind, hahahaha don't ask, byeeeeeee, Jimmy, the Salesman of the Century.

Ps
Can you use Madonna's boutier or Simon Cowell's old T-shirt that he wore on 'American Idol' well I can get 'em, just tell me what you want and when, I can make it happen cos I'm the handy man!!!

Folks, like those Sandford characters I tried out for a part in a new show where they were looking for some newly undiscovered talented actors, well me being a heck of an actor I knew I would fit in just right. So I mosey on over to that studio behind the alley way and I walk in and introduce myself and after giving me the once over they had me fill out an application but the questions they were asking were a wee bit odd, like how long could I hold it up and how big was my Johnny boy. So I asked what's a Johnny boy, and the folks there all looked at me and smiled. Then they asked did I have a portfolio of my works. What works, you said undiscovered hunks that's all I have to show but I was once a rooster in an all you can eat chicken buffet restaurant and I was in a Shakespeare play back in the 6th grade and that's when I recited some of the lines. Here check it out "TO BE OR NOT TO BE THAT IS THE QUESTION, AND JULIET JULIET WHERE ART THOU WOMAN, IT IS I, YOUR ROMEO." Next they wanted me to undress to my shorts so I figured I was going to put on a costume and that's when they asked me to walk so I strutted my stuff and they just went gaga, no not Lady Ga Ga, ga ga like I was too much ga ga. Well I was finally told I was accepted for lead role in an X-rated movie. Then I said a porno movie, what's in it for me, lots of money, girls, and all the meat you can eat. I stormed out of there cos I'm a vegetarian, 100% pure all whole wheat, ciao, Jimmy

Hey guys have you ever told that woman what you really think of her, well you're in luck cos the love man is going to show you how. First of all put on this Keith Urban song, words like I wanna sleep with, die in your arms, and love her like nobody has, I guarantee you she will be blown away. You see a woman needs more than just gifts, she wants attention and to be told how much you love her. Oh the gifts are ok if you can afford them but if you can't a candle lit dinner for two, soft sweet romantic music will be the start of a blissful night of passion. I should know that woman seduces me every night come December and you know what happens. I burst at the seams every time, oh, how I love that little girl of mine, well if this doesn't do it for you nothing will and my suggestion read some books. The Joy of Sex, 9 ½ weeks, 50 Shades Of Gray and so forth. Ciao got something very important to tell her, ok ok I'll tell you, I love you pussy cat, I do! Jimmy

Keith Urban—Making Memories of Us

Yes I am, that song is all me and I can be yours if the price is right, how's that, well if you want some of this you got to give some of that and not only that, your money too. Why's that, cos I've been accustomed to only the best, the best restaurants, the best vacations, the best clothes, the best cars that your money can buy. What's in it for you, good question glad you asked, me, all of me, 100% hunk. When I get you in my arms I will squeeze you to death. You will think you died and went to heaven in a Rolls Royce, see I told you only the best. And you can start calling me Boss or Lover Man, hahahaha. Byeeeeeee, got an appointment at the tailors, getting me a spanking new outfit, no you can't spank me, well not yet, show me the money first hahahaha

Jane Olivor—He's So Fine

Folks I got some great news when you buy my book you are automatically entered in a drawing for a chance to win 'my Pussy in a box to go.' What's so special about that little lady? Good question, she's the best bug repellant ever and will rid you of mice and or rats from your home or I'll eat Pookie in a Macys store window. But that's not all and here's the best part, when it's freaking cold outside she'll keep your feet toasty hot. Oh you haven't heard the end you can kick her around the house and she'll always come back to you. So tell me what woman or man you know does all those things for you, that's right, nada, zero, zilch and it proves who needs a spouse when you got her. What, what am I going to do without her, have you ever heard of three dog night, yep when it's cold outside I'll be sleeping with three dogs, What can I say, I'm brighter than a light bulb, ciao Jimmy!!!!

I remember it like if it were yesterday I was in love, ok so I was only 5 but I was and she was in my kindergarten class and when I heard she was moving away I just wanted to die, it broke my heart in two. Well this song reminds me of that little girl and the way I felt deep inside my soul for her. Enjoy it and please when you hear it think of me. What became of her, she moved two blocks away but I was happy like a pig in slop, love that girl to death, byeeeeeeeeee, Jimmy
James Carr—To Love Somebody

Folks I got a story you're just not going to believe, you remember when my Irish friend Mickey introduced me to some of the boys down at the firehouse, Squad 288 here in Maspeth, last year well they all took a liking to me, especially Captain Longhorn and they asked me if I would like to join their fraternity band of brothers cos they could see I was all that and a bag of chips. And get this; they even wanted me to be their mascot at the St. Paddy's Day Parade here in NY in front of millions of people and on National TV, their first ever, mascot that is. But they also wanted me to do two things which I found quite strange, be the last man in the parade, and to wear a kilt when we march down on 5th Avenue, and last but not least moon the folks as we marched down. Now I don't know why I couldn't march alongside of them, no, they say it's an honor to be the closer. They always pick an Irish celebrity to lead the parade and that I should be at the end, this way we would have both ends covered. But I don't see the lead guy mooning anybody the way they wanted me to. They said my job was the most important part of the parade so to be part of this awesome group of guys I decided to do it, why not; these are America's finest, the brave men and women of the NYC Fire Department. How did it go, I thought you'd never ask, I was the laughing stock of the parade and to make matters worse I was later arrested for indecent exposure. And when I went to jail none of the guys showed up in my defense, not even did they chip in to post my bail. When we went to court the judge wanted to know why had I done what I had done and when I explained how I was chosen to be their first mascot ever and become one of their band of brothers he said I was lied to and that he would suspend the charges for time already served, fourteen days, and for being a nincompoop. The nerve of him calling me that, he should have said I was a hero in the line of duty, who else would have done what I had done. Now whenever I go to the fire house they all gather around smiling from ear to ear and laughing hysterically and say I'm the man. So I say to them, than if I'm the man can I do sleepovers and polish up their bells and they all agreed I could. How many days have I stayed over in the firehouse, not a freaking day, they always seem to have an excuse of some kind, like the Fire Commissioner is in town, or they're having an inspection, or they're going to paint up the fire house but something tells me they don't want me over. Well I'm still proud to say I'm a part of them no matter what. Ciao and do enjoy Ben E. King, he too was lied to but who cares, bye bye, Jimmy
Ben E. King—Don't Play That Song

See the four replies I got back . . .

To come up with all these stories it takes some brain, sometimes I wander if you have more than one brain . . . The funny part is that I can imagine you at the parade mooning everybody . . . hahaha.

And here I was thinking I was crazy, ha! But that was before I knew you. Thank you for the share, never heard this song, don't tell anybody that. Have a great rest of weekend and a very happy day! Big hug, Alma

ahahahahahahahahahahahahahahahahahahahahahaha you were arrested for indecent exposure. ya mooner you . . . hahahahahahahahahahahahahahahahahahahahahahahaha

I would love to have seen it . . . it would have been like all my Christmases come at once and you are a bona fide member of the MacNumpty clan, Now that means you got to come round my house and show me what you got, no, not the family jewels, your kilt, hahaha
Ps
Nothing is worn under the kilt, why? because everything is in perfect working order hahaha bye

You're welcome Jimmy, your stories are fabulozaaaaaaaaa wow you write little mini novels in your messages to us all. I love all your stories, but appreciated this one very much.
(see I watch a lot of American TV) hahaha

Folks I got something to tell you I'm thinking of expanding my horizons and running for some kind of political office. If you really must know politicians are the most corrupted people on the face of the earth, they vote themselves big fat raises, they travel the world, eat at the finest restaurants all at the taxpayer's expenses and best of all, always scratching each other's butts. That's why I would do well cos I can be just as corrupted as the next guy. I'm an ass kisser by heart; love to hold babies and that sort of stuff. I'll get my friends and family members all hooked up with high paying jobs that require nothing or very little to do. Well I was hoping you would all vote for me, they'll be something in it for you. A chicken in every pot, sexy girls and guys and all the booze you can drink. My inauguration will be the most unforgettable. I'll hire a bunch of strippers, male and female, so you can get your whistle wet or whatever else needs wetting and that definitely goes for you girls. Maybe we party separately and I'll take you for a whirlwind don't ask. So remember to vote for me but I'm leaving it all up to you, ciao, Jimmy, aka senator, mayor, governor, president, who knows just call me god while you're at it cos I'm Taylor made and schooled by those Tammany Hall scoundrels c ya hate to be ya . . .
Mr. Smith Goes to Washington (1939)—James Stewart

Here's a reply to die for, enjoy, Jimmy

Wooo, corrupt, ass licking butt wiping horny good for nothing, whistle wetting, sexual deviant politicians. Haven't they all been Presidents of the US ? hahaha Maggie

Ladies I'm throwing a garage sale, this will be my 13th on record. You're aware I was married 13 times well every time we parted ways I would do the gentlemanly thing and show them out to the curb and then instead of discarding all their shit I would convert their goods into cold hard cash, that's right, get rid of all their belongings. Stuff that I had purchased for

them, things like negligees, furs, shoes, dresses, suits, blouses you name it, it had to go. If you must know when we separated, no correct that, when I threw them out the door head first it was without a stitch of anything, the way they came in is the way they went out. So come one, come all, and you know the early worm catches the bird or some shit. I got all the name brands, Donna Karen, Alfani, Nine West, Holston, Calvin Klein, Gucci, Oscar de la Renta, Stella McCartney, Tommy Hilfiger, Versace, even got some Lady Ga Ga replicas. Everything must go, and drastically reduced, half off or better, that's right and they'll all one of a kind, had them goods altered and made by them there fashion designers. Hope to see you there, you'll walk in empty handed and go out a rich bitch, hahahaha
Buster Poindexter—Hit The Road Jack

I got to ask you a question, is it me or do you do the same thing, whenever I pay a visit to a hospital I cover myself all up. I not only put on a face mask but I wear one of those hospital gowns cos you never know what you're going to get. Think about it, who are those folks in a hospital, yep sick people and what is it that sick people got, right again germs. So I don't want what they got, I press that elevator button only if I have to otherwise I press it with a knuckle. I play it smart let the folks in first and hope and pray somebody has already pressed the floor I'm going to otherwise I cringe and do that knuckle press. It's not being rude it's being careful so if you ever happen to go to a hospital be on your guard cos you surely don't want to have to be a patient cos you caught some kind of disease and it might even kill ya. You know hospitals are not a ball where you go in to have a good time please please be careful and use protection and definitely don't come a knocking to my house cos I'm not in, ciao Jimmy

Folks I got a story to tell ya that you're just not going to believe, I read all the obituaries and I look for opportunities whenever the right moment arises. I make my way over to that dead person's home and pretend to be a long lost lover. I don't do it with just anybody, somebody who was childless and there's only a sibling or two cos then I can get what I'm after, their money and belongings. I say we were lovers some 20-30 years ago and our only child died at birth. I know it sounds crazy well if she's dead what good is her money and valuables I might as well get some or all of it. Hey do you know anybody who just died and was fully loaded, no not that kind of loaded, what do you think I am, a pervert, don't answer that!!!

Way to go Eddie Murphy, see folks if you give in next thing you know he will have you washing his draws and socks. You got to stand up and show him you aint no sissy man. I would kick his ass while he's sleeping so when he gets out of the hospital he knows better to mess with a looney bird cos next time I'd chew him up and bury the mother sucker. Enjoy the clipping and go see the movie in its entirety I know I am, ciao Jimmy
Martin Lawrence & Eddie Murphy—Life

Folks I dedicate this song to one special gal out there; don't ask me to reveal her name cos this is one secret I want to share only between us. She drives me insane and I can't stop thinking of her. All I know when we are together it's a five alarm fire cos the mere presence of her omg you don't want to know. She melts me away I just go bonkers and all I want to do is hold and squeeze her and tell her what she means to me . . . . Jimmy

Johnny Mathis—It's Not For Me To Say

Did you say get tired of you, girl I would walk on water, fight a hungry bear to make you mine and if that's not enough climb the highest mountain on the face of the earth, Mt. Kilimanjaro or Mt. Everest whichever is the tallest and swim the Atlantic Ocean from NY to Gay Paris cos than you would know what you mean to me, you're my love, my Baby Girl . . . Forever yours, Jimmy
The Association—Never My Love

Let me learn you something about cornbread, when I was up the river on my third visit I had to set a bunch of low life mother suckers that you don't mess with the kid, that's me, the kid, cos if you let your guard down just once they will own you. I had to be tough and take no lip or shit from no one and the bigger they were the more you had to be crazy cos that was my way out. If you want to earn respect you got to be crazy, no I mean you got to look the part, and play the part. The very first day this big ugly mo-fo came up to me and wanted my corn bread, that was the first and last time anybody wanted my corn bread cos I shoved my size 10 and a half up his ass and then while he was down I kicked him some more and to this day he's washes my clothes. So you see you got to act crazy when you're in a bind, do what the crazy folks do: scream, holler, bite, and scratch their eyes out, rip their noses and ears off and they will never ever bother you again. Yep I'm crazier than a fox, you don't want to know, ciao Jimmy aka Killer\
Martin Lawrence & Eddie Murphy—Life

I just thought of a new game plan to make a ton of money, instead of that extension six feet out I dig six feet down and this way I can bury the dead. Yeah I'll be a mortician and a gravedigger all in one. I know lots of people who are looking to save a bundle on funeral expenses so I give them the cheapest funeral out there. Today it cost on an average about nine thousand dollars to get buried. I'll charge three thousand, and if they want I can cremate them for even less, fifteen hundred but between you and me I won't, I'll get me some dust and fill that urn to the brim and just bury that body along with the rest. You've heard that expression from dust to dust hahahaha and guess what, I'll save on the extras too. Like no hearse for one, nor a minister, heck I can say a few good words my daddy the preacher man used to tell me, and there'll be no need for flowers cos there's a bunch of trees back there and when the mourners leave I throw the body into that pit, who's going to be the wiser, hahaha. And when that pit has about fifty bodies in it, close to the top, I throw in those bags of cement I was bringing home; about ten bags should do the trick. See already I'm saving twenty bags of cement then I go out to the parks late at night and bury the newly dead folks there. Girl I should have thought of this long ago, I'd be driving my Porsche and hobnobbing with the rich folk, my new peers, ta ta, got to get my shovel and oil it up. What's ta ta, oh that's what the British folk say when it's time to say good bye. Me, I think it has another meaning; the British folk are nasty hahahaha I just know what they really mean . . .
Blood, Sweat & Tears—And When I Die

Got to tell you something, see that video by The Marvelows singing "I Do," well guess what, "I Do." You see the kid, that's moi, that means 'me' in French or in Hindu or some shit, I'm in love, and this time it's for real and if I play my cards right she will be number fourteen. What's that, she'll not only be wearing my ring but will be carrying my last name? Now the hard part, her daddy is one SOB, and maybe I'll email him for permission for her hand. Why email, cos this way he can't kill me. You see I got a reputation for being a ladies man and my persona is I'm a hunk and his daughter is his pride and joy. And to know I'm the man who stole her away from him will leave a crushing blow to his ego. Hey he should be lucky I don't whip his ass but that's not my style anymore, how else did I survive this long after stealing those other thirteen gals, well it was really eleven, wife number 2, 7, and 11 were the same gal, she just had to have me over and over and over, once was not enough. Well enjoy the song and do remember me cos I'm the hunter and my hunger is ferocious hahahahahaha

The Marvelows—I Do

Now you can add 'insurance con man' to my distinguished resume, BAM!!!! And btw it was me who came up with that phrase first not Emeril Lagasse he just copied me when we used to party together. Well never mind that let me tell you how I earned that title 'insurance con man.' A few days ago me and the boys were playing poker, oh we get together every weekend, drink some beers, watch the fights, and play for heavy stakes, usually there's two or three hundred dollars on the table, not bad for eight or nine guys. Well on Saturday last I had noticed Santiago Morales was a little bit stiff so I asked him what was the matter and he told me he was in a car accident. While sitting in his car at a stop sign he was struck from behind by a Cadillac by some guy named Jonathan Trump. So that's when Sally 'Salvatore' Bonanno says you're sitting on a goldmine so that's when I chimed in, yep and if you play your cards right I can make you rich. You should have seen Santiago's eyes light up. So he says, how's that, I say, what hit you, a Cadillac, who was driving it, a white rich man by the name of Trump. So I tell Santiago I got an old neck brace thingy and a cane and a walker, starting today and every day I want you to use them and I'll get my lawyer Alma Albright to represent you in a whip lash case. That babe is hot, no not hot that way, hot that she never loses a case, but then what do I know if she's hot in the sack hahahaha. By the time we're finished with him, Jonathan Trump, we'll own one of the Trump Buildings and it'll be 50, 25, 25. So Santiago says I get 50, I and I say no, I get the 50. Who came up with the scheme, me, who's going to give you the neck brace, the cane, and the walker, me, and then Santiago says "oh." Well folks that's how my insurance con days started, so if you know somebody just recently hurt, send them my way and you'll get a finder's fee, how much, ten bucks. Hey, I'll keep you abreast on the case. Pardon me, but next time you hear from me I will be saying "**I Park My Car By The Harbor**," yes I will be rolling in the dough and girls galore every which way I go, farewell Jimmy and from now on, it's Mr. Jimmy to you!!!

Sanford and Son—Whiplash

Hey Sweet Pies have you ever heard of the song "Special Lady" by Ray, Goodman, & Brown well for the life of me I never knew what "pop pop goes the weasel" meant. I know one thing when I put on this song I just want to slow dance and you just know I'll be popping cos that girl in front of me has me in heaven sitting on top of the world alright. Hey, if you know what that means "pop pop goes the weasel" tell me I'm dying to know. We lost Ray and Goodman but their legacy will long live on. I'm about ready to pop, don't ask, hahaha, have a good one, Jimmy

Ray, Goodman, & Brown—Special Lady

Have you ever been sad and blue, of course you have, I've been there and done that many a times but it's not the end of the world. How I overcome these drastic feelings is in one of two ways. First of all I count my blessings, did I lose a limb, my eye sight, a family member, my house burnt down, my car totaled, lost my wallet, well maybe one of those things did happen but did all of them happen to you or a loved one. Ok so you had a spat with a loved one and maybe they met someone new well lucky for them but that's not a reason to get down on yourself. Like that song by The Marvelettes "Too Many Fish In The Sea," You'll find another, and maybe this time it'll be a barracuda or a handsome shark. What's the other thing; I put on a comedy movie or read a funny book to make me laugh, to make me forget but most of all to lift my spirits. Home Alone, Planes, Trains, & Automobiles, or a Steve Martin, a Martin Lawrence, a John Candy, or a Tom Hanks movie, oh I could name another dozen or so actors and movies. You see I was once very sick and depressed and when I saw Joe Pesci being beaten up by Kevin, aka Macaulay Culkin, I died laughing and before I knew it I recovered in no time. So please don't beat yourself up, hey come over to my channel and go through my jimmyscomedyshop Revisited Playlist and it will cure what ails you, I promise you that, ciao, Jimmy

When I was in school Charlie Brown was my idol and everybody wanted to be just like him. He was delinquent's greatest gift to schools, why the man singlehandedly drove the teachers and principals insane with his antics. We would have spit ball parties and when he spoke it was more like wtf did he say cos with his daddio lingo we never fully understood what he was saying. I can recall whenever a teacher lectured to him his replies drove them mad, all he would say was "huh." Oh they wanted to kill him right there and then but I guess too many witnesses. I mean the man could do no wrong he would do graffiti on the walls, like "Eat At Joe's, or at your mama's." Or when he thought the building was way too hot he'd pull the fire alarm so all the kids could catch a breather when they had to evacuate the building. When we went to gym he would always find an excuse not to build up a sweat, like I banged my toe in the auditorium or my house burnt down last night so I didn't get enough sleep, so wake me when it's time to go home, I mean the man was crazy like a fox and smarter than a fifth grader. Enjoy The Coasters!!
The Coasters—Charlie Brown

Can you keep a secret, my uncle Chavos, first name Gimme, was a great painter, I mean in the same level as Guillermo da Vinci, Chopin, and Ernesto Hemingway. It was he who got me all those art scholarships. How, good question, he would draw something and then add numbers to it, so all I would have to do is add in the colors and presto I had a masterpiece of my own. My works are displayed all over town. At the museum of Natural History, the YMCA, heck even the Trumps and Bloomberg's got me hanging up on their walls. I will go down in history as the greatest forger of them all. Hey you want to own a little bit of me, send me 100 thousand dollars, in USD, no yens, or pesos, or pounds, nor euros and I'm all yours. Ciao I'm due at the art class, I'm their nude model today, wooooo hooooo money money money, byeeeeee, Jimmy

Some people have special talents well if you really must know I'm blessed with a bunch of them but here's one I never told anybody. I talk to angels and they kind of like what I say. I give them ideas and pointers. You see I know who needs help; Charlie Sheen like one

needs plenty of that. Now if you be good to me I'll tell them to watch over you and yes you will straighten up. How do I know, I've straightened up myself, look at me now, I'm a star and when I get that star on the ground there in Hollywood everybody's going to know my name, call me when you're ready for when you want some of this, yes me, hahahaha. Ciao and how Jimmy, your man
Black Crowes—She Talks To Angels

I got to tell you something, when you are feeling blue cos you and your lover boy aren't talking for whatever reason well I got a solution to your troubles but let me tell you a story first. When I was out of the box, you know, beginning to date, I was just six years old. Well at that point in time I met the most beautiful creature this side of heaven, I think she was five and we got to talking, and before you knew it we got to walking and soon I asked her to be my girl. After a long pause, five seconds at the most, she said yes. Well we were an item every day for the next three months but then I had my shoe shine business to take care of and she was mad at me cos she couldn't bear to be without me not even for an hour. Well this song by Champaign will further explain my situation. Girl did I love that girlie so. What became of her, she's a stripper in a nightclub act somewhere in Paris, I visit her every chance I get and she still loves to walk and talk and do other things, mums the word, a gentleman never tells, hahahaha enjoy Champaign they too have a solution to any spat, they just try again and again and again, ciao Jimmy. Got to get me some roses, you guessed it, for that little girlie of mine . . . .
Champagne—Try Again

Check out this reply below.

Re: Champagne Try Again. From the moment you said you were—only six years old—you had me laughing so hard, couldn't even concentrate to the rest of the story, I had to read it again . . . very sweet :) Usually boys' first love is one of their teachers, but then again you are not one of the usual boys . . . hahaha, yes, of course it's a compliment :) Thank you and have a great day, Hugs, Alma

For those who don't know I am the reincarnation of James Dean, who is James Dean, good question, he was the baddest movie star that ever lived, why he could make the womenfolk drool and put the fear in men. Well it was he who started me on my career of terror and that was when I was seven years old in the third grade. I was so bad my teacher would put me in front of the class standing facing the corner of the room. Well that didn't stop me that just got me started, I would do crazy things, you don't want to know. Ok, ok, I would scratch my butt, cut wind, and I mean good and loud, and I would say pardon me, and the class would start laughing hysterically and the teacher couldn't do a thing cos who do you know doesn't fart, we're all humans and shit does happen. But the truth is I can fart at command I guess I have a talent for that too, you don't believe me, here, pull my thumb and see what happens hahahaha. Another thing I would do when the teacher had to leave the room for any type of emergency. I would gather up all the blackboard erasers and chuck them out the window. The kids knew better then to squeal on me cos I would beat them silly after school if they dared and they would get two black eyes to show for their good deeds. So when the teacher would come back in to resume her lessons everybody was holding their breath waiting in anticipation for when she would have to erase the board and when that time did arise the whole class would burst in tears laughing and she knew right there and then I was the culprit responsible. Omg you should have seen her chasing me around that classroom and she would be in tears and I think she would have strangled me if she had caught up to me. Sure enough the next day I was suspended from class until my mother showed up and as a result I would get the beating of my life, but then that's why I was called a rebel rouser, badder than ole King Kong. Hey, enjoy James Dean

David Essex—Rock On

Another funny reply, enjoy, Jimmy.

Re: Rock on!—Jimmy Dean. Omg you made me laugh in tears again, I love stories about school and those years of our lives that will stay with us forever even though they are so far behind. James Dean was born in the same year with my mom and died before I was born. I haven't seen a single movie with him; all I knew about him was that he died very young and that he was handsome. Loved the video, thank you for the share :)

Take care, Alma

Hey you remember that monkey story I told you about a few weeks back, yeah my pet for ransom business idea, don't remind me. I'm thinking of getting me one and attach it to an organ push cart or wachamacallit and I charge folks for my visit, like for a birthday party, a hen party, a school reunion, sweet 16, holiday celebration, a wedding, a divorce celebration, whatever. Now the only problem is where am I going to get a monkey and it's got to be a new born so I can train it to do my beckoning call. The thought of me going over to Africa, or the everglades of Spain will no doubt cost me a bundle and I already spent a ton of money after that other monkey destroyed my house. I was thinking of going to zoos and kidnap me one, yeah I climb over the fence but before I do that I give the mama monkey bananas filled with sleeping pills, oh about 15 pills in each banana and when she doses off I snatch me her baby. I know what a great idea. I'll keep you in the loop as to my progress, and I just know this is going to make me a fistful of dollars. Why you ask, well this will be my plan 'B' in case my books don't sell. I know it a brilliant idea it's so original. Hey that reminds me, enjoy the Originals with their hit song "Baby I'm For Real" and so is that baby monkey that I'm going to snatch hahaha. Wish me luck, Jimmy

The Originals—Baby I'm For Real

I got an embarrassing story to reveal but you must promise me you'll never utter a word of what I'm about to say, that monkey business idea was a terrible idea. Let me start from the beginning. Last week I told you I wanted to get a monkey and an organ cart and charge folks for the entertainment I was going to provide them for any and every occasion and how I was going to kidnap me a newborn monkey from a zoo. Well when I was just about to put that plan into motion I realized I only had enough sedated bananas for six monkeys when there were 10 of them in that big ole cage. So I aborted and had to get four more sedated bananas filled with 15 pills each. The next day I come fully prepared, 30 bananas with 15 sleeping pills in each for a grand total of 450 pills and let me remind you that was a costly bill, don't remind me, a dollar a pill, 450 dollars in all. So I start climbing that picket fence and when I reached to the top I got pricked in my butt, pardon the pun. As I gently get off I

jump over that alligator ditch and finally get to where the monkeys were sleeping. And as I try to grab the newborn it wouldn't let go of its mothers tit, it's stuck light gorilla glue so I lay down next to the mother monkey and I pull and twist with all my might but that's when the mother monkey rolls over right on top of me. Omg what am I to do. Then the mother monkey in its dead of sleep thinks I'm her mate and prepares to do it's mating ritual. It grips me good and tight and starts rocking back and forth like a rocking robin on a tree top. After 10 minutes of continuous fast thrusting motions it reaches climax and it's smiling from ear to ear and finally releases me. I jumped off and ran for the hills without that newborn, by this time I don't care nor want that gorilla anymore. Plus it would take me a year or more for that monkey to learn to push that cart with me on top playing the accordion organ so it's a done deal. Please don't mention this; can you see the headlines now, monkey and man getting it on? Hey it doesn't count cos it takes two to tangle and I did no tangling, end of story, period, finito. In the meantime enjoy Rockin Robin, ciao, Jimmy
Bobby Day—Rockin Robin

Do you ever have nightmare dreams or is it just me, well I do all the time but it was much worse when I was a kid. See every time I watched a horror movie, like Count Dracula, The Wolf Man, Frankenstein, The Mummy, The Invisible Man I would be so afraid when I went to bed that I had to close all the windows and arm myself with a machete or a big ole rock I found out in the back yard and brought into the house in case I needed to whack that Bat aka Bela Lugosi or The Wolf Man, aka Lon Chaney Jr. I would be so afraid that I would wet the bed but please don't tell nobody cos at the age of 8 or 9 a boy that age aint supposed to be peeing in the bed otherwise I would be the laughing stock in the neighborhood. So tell me, did you or are you still having them kind of nightmare dreams. Girl it can stump your growth, I'm 3 feet 9 inches short and I'm sure I should have been at least a foot taller but these crazy dreams did me in, what say you and do you enjoy Frankenstein he was a terror, don't remind me, ciao, Jimmy

When I was in grammar school the teacher would send my mother letters but I would open them up and if it said anything bad about me I would tear them up. Miss Rachett, yes that was my teacher's name got wise to me and mailed my mother a telegram asking both of us to come to the principal's office regarding my erratic behavior. And here we are in the principal's office and right there in front of me she has the audacity to tell my mother I was never going to amount to anything. Oh you aint heard the last, when we get home my mother pulls out my daddy's leather buckled motorcycle belt and whips me to a pulp. Well I got news for Miss Rachett where ever you are, I fooled them all. Look at me now, I've written a book, not just any book, a best seller. I sold ten copies today and 8 the day before and god only knows how many tomorrow and all you can do is read it, so put that in your pipe and smoke it you slime ball hahahahaha. Moral of the story, don't mess with Jim, and in the meantime enjoy that other Jim, ciao Jimmy . . .
Jim Croce—You Don't Mess Around With Jim

I know you heard by now, I've written a tell all tale book about my YT experiences, well it's true but I must admit I had a lot of accomplices but I rather keep their names anonymous to protect the innocent. You can purchase that book through amazon.com, iUniverse.com, or simply place an order at your local book store including Barnes and Noble and search under my name Jimmy Correa or the title of the book (HOW MY PRANK STORIES IN 'YOU TUBE' MADE ME AN OVERNIGHT SENSATION) ciao and do enjoy this video my first ever, thanks Jimmy

Ps
I can't lie, I had a little help, Pookie helped me along she told me how and where to put it, no not that you silly goose, my fingers and hands on all the parts and knobs on my hard drive and look what the cat brought in, a first class video, fuhgettaboudit . . .

I was once told I have the gift for gab, well I don't know if that's true but I do I like telling it like it is. What is gift for gab, that's someone who talks and talks, and talks and doesn't shut up, hahahaha sounds familiar, well that's you too. I've made a lot of good friends in YT and some send me things and then some. One gal in particular makes me videos, another one sends me jokes, and yet another wants to own me, and another wants to stone me, hahaha. Well then maybe I do have that gift and I want to tell you a story. My grandmother once tried to commit suicide. You see my grandfather was out of his mind and killed himself. Upon hearing this grandmother asked how he died, well nobody wanted to tell her so I stepped up to the plate and told her he shot himself under the left nipple. The next day my grandmother was rushed to the hospital. She too tried to shoot herself under the left nipple and shot her knee cap, now she uses a motor chair scooter to get around. You should see her pop wheelies, oh well that's life, ciao, Jimmy

Ps
You got to see her pop wheelies, enjoy Joe Jones with his story of someone with the gift of gab
Joe Jones—You Talk Too Much (1960)

Can you keep another secret, I still confide in my fortune teller, every week I go over to her office, that's what she calls it now but it's just a small room in her house 6 by 6 to have a consultation, if you ask me it looks like a broom closet. What's a consultation, wtf do I know, she calls our readings that, and I think it makes her feel important like as if she were a doctor with a PHD? Last night I paid her a visit, and she told me I was going to hit the mother lode so I asked her what did she mean by that and she gave me that one eyed evil look, yeah she wears a patch on the other, and said sucker you're going to be mingling with the rich and famous. Then I smiled and said oooooooo weeeeeeee. At first I thought was I going to meet a hot mama, you know fully loaded, and then I begin to read in between the lines and realized I'm going to be rich and famous. You do know I wrote a blockbuster YT book, what's a blockbuster, that's when you sell a lot of books a couple of hundred or more and people start calling you sir. Has it happened yet, no but I know it's going to happen one day soon. Well I got to go my agent is calling me, that jerk probably wants some more money, I pay her by the week, and she gets plenty of me, don't ask hahaha, byeeeeeeeeeeee, Jimmy, aka the Pulitzer Prize I know it going to happen author

I got a story that will curdle your toes, I met a girl the other day as I was picking tomatoes at my local supermarket veggie stand and she came up to me and asked me if I could help her pick melons, so I says to her, didn't your mother tell you it's not proper to speak to strangers and then she told me she was an alien sent down to find a husband to beget babies. Well you know me, I told her I could give you some babies come on over to my crib and I'll show you a good time and sock it too ya. That's when her eyes lit up like a light bulb. And besides I couldn't pass up a good opportunity to see what she had, she being an alien I just had to see how they make 'em in them other planets, and besides I'm only doing this for the betterment of mankind and to make peace. Her eyes lit up, no really they did so I told her I too was a space alien, and when she asked where from, I told her from Passthefuss, it's one light year away. Well the minute we walked into my house she removed her clothing and before I could say 'howdy' she was all over me. I must say I thought earth girls were easy well she was faster than a speeding bullet and she had the biggest and sexiest pair I've ever seen, eyes, eyes get your mind out of the gutter. Well how was your day, good as mine I hope? Jimmy

Have you ever had high hopes on things you thought were impossible and then you worked your fingers to the bone and achieved your goals. Well that's what happened to me cos I'm a fighter through and through, let me explain. I was once strolling on the beach one Sunday morning minding my own business when this foxy little girl just happened to be walking my way when we caught eyes. So I decided right there and then she had to be mine. So I park right behind her to try to win her love. I began to dig a ditch and build a sand castle three feet by ten feet and after two hours of hard labor I completed it and I asked her to join me. Heck I even spread open my towel so she could lay and play in it with me. She was so impressed with the kid that I decided to ask her for her number and address and we became the best of friends. She was 8 and I was 9, hahaha. No, we did not get married but we sure partied for many a summer in that sand castle for two, just she and I.
Frank Sinatra—High Hopes

When I was a kid I would watch an episode of 'The Little Rascals' every morning before going off to school. It was about a bunch of kids just like all kids growing up and facing the world probably no different than when you or I were kids. Well I always got to school late as a result. The teacher would say "what this time Jimmy" and I would always find an excuse. Like my mother lost my homework but lucky for me I found it in her cookie jar. See I was a con man/kid back then too. Well it's this episode that caused me to run away from home and join the circus. At first I would be cleaning up after the elephants and then the tigers, then the gorillas. But then my break came through when the headliner of The Flying Trapeze artist came down with an unexpected bout of scurvy. I wonder what could have brought that upon him hahaha, yep it was me, I added some elephant you know what into his soup and he got sick, poor boy hahaha. So I volunteered to go up. And that was the start of my new profession, the greatest Trapeze artist of all time. Maybe you of heard of me, Don Jimmy & his Flying Deuces. Enjoy The Little Rascals and think of me if you should ever get to see them in your neck of the woods, ciao Jimmy
The Little Rascals—The International Silver String Submarine Band

Love this reply below, enjoy, Jimmy

Re: The International Silver String Submarine Band. Yep from when you were knee high to a grasshopper you were a con kid progressing to con man and with a face like your icon the circus was the best place for you. Elephant you-know-what in his soup. jeeez he must have lost his sense of smell and you must have lost your marbles.

Wow I wish I`d seen you in action. Jimmy The Lover Man & His Flying Deuces . . . sounds more like a pop group that a circus act . . . . Did you know I once worked on the trapeze at a circus too, so I know the ropes . . . haha
Maggie

Did you know Rod Stewart and I have many things in common, no it's true, we were both grave diggers in our past, don't remind me. I buried people on the download, yep I killed them as a hit contract, he on the other hand buried them for a living cos they needed to be buried or rigor mortis would set in, you know you get hard, no not that kind of hard hahaha, and also the foul smell would kill you too. Another thing we have in common he collects models and so do I; but mine I hang up on the walls while he beds them to death. And yes we're both very sexy but that you already know; well don't you remember when I told you I was a hunk, from head to toe. Enjoy "Do You Think I'm Sexy," thank you, Jimmy
Rod Stewart—Do You Think I'm Sexy

Check out this funny reply below.

Re: Da Ya Think I'm Sexy? The "para bing para bang" made me laugh in tears, you crazy man, you. When I bought "Guinness Book of Records" I knew there was something to read more interesting than anything else . . . so that was you!? Is your middle name "crazy"? Mine too!
Have I ever told you that I love your sense of humor, yeah, probably at least a dozen times? Thank you for the share :) Have a great day, hugs,
Alma

That's the incomparable Billy Joel singing his ass off who had the uncanny ability to sing in any style of any decade he chooses to portray, the fifties, the sixties or in the present and still make it a big hit. Like in his lyrics we all wanted to be that character he sang about cos they were our heroes. I recall how I wanted to ditty bop and yes stickball was our formal education cos I could hit that ball silly sailing two or three sewers away. And if that wasn't enough we were the big shots and we could be right or wrong but that's who we were. Boy was he 100% right on the money and street savvy and I'm sure he didn't hang with any wild boys nor made love to any red head in a Chevrolet well at least not until he made it big and bought a whole slew of cars, but I'm certain he wouldn't want to go into details being the gentleman that he is especially with his uptown girls. Hey his history lesson is to die for so while you're here enjoy all his other songs and sing-a-long that's a must, ciao, Jimmy
Billy Joel—Keeping The Faith/ You May Be Right/ My Life/ We Didn't Start The Fire

I got a story to tell you, have you ever heard of the 'Dodo Bird,' it was thought to have disappeared from the face of the earth back in the sixteen hundreds and were put on the extinct list. Well I got some good news and some bad news to report. The good news first, it's no longer on the extinct list. Now for the bad news, there's a bunch of them nesting at my job sight and they haven't changed a bit, lazy and dumb as ever. I'm going to inform 'Wild Kingdom' and 'National Geographic Society' to put them back on the still active list. Going to send them the proof and it won't look pretty; one ugly bunch is how I see them. Check Ian Bernardo he too has spotted one or more, ciao Jimmy

Ian Bernardo—American Idol

Now this reply is mean yet so true, hahahaha

Re: Ian Bernardo No the Dodo Bird is alive and well . . . just watched him on a video you shared . . . hahaha, missy

Only in America and better than that, made in America is what I am and where else can a poor boy like me grow up to be endowed and with so many skills and opportunities. Oh there were hills and valleys I've had to overcome and I've been up and down but never out. I've shoveled elephant shit when I worked my way through the circus. I've picked cotton, don't ask, and now I wear the finest clothing money can buy, guess jeans, gap suits made in China and Payless alligator shoes from Timbuktu. I've had escorts up to the ying yang and everybody calls me sir or boss. I've dined with kings and hoboes, OJ and even J Lo. I've been around the world from Alaska to Pottawattamie. My walls are covered with works of art and everybody knows my name. Heck I might even run for president and then they'll be calling me King. Hey enjoy Jay & The Americans they too are from you guessed it, America, ciao and how.
Sir Jimmy

Did I tell you I was once a hot shot on Wall Street? What happened I lost it all in the market back in 2008, my stock broker tricked me into buying a piece of the rock. Yeah I bought everything he told me and now I'm flat broke and he's a fat cat mingling with the upper class in some brothel in old Mexico. Well enough of that I know better this time. I'll spread it out, keep some in my pillow, in my mattress, in the oven, bury some in the back yard, up on the roof, in my basement, and in a safe behind that picture of Pamela Anderson. My agent says I should buy a Picasso, is he crazy that would take all his money and mine put together just for one piece of art, no way. I want something I can feel. Well you won't have to worry cos that's just the beginning. I'll buy some hot commodities; gold, silver, and copper, a herd of cows, bulls, chickens, some oil wells, futures of OJ, no not him, orange juice, and some underground gas. I'll be rich but I can't get discouraged cos sometimes it has to go down but then it has to go up, don't ask, in the meantime enjoy "For The Love Of Money" by The O' Jays

I remember I was at the beach with a bunch of friends, I must have been 16 or 17, and we were playing two hand touch football, you know the American sport of that oblong ball well as we were playing this girl was falling down and tried to hold on to me, but accidentally grabbed onto my bathing suit as she fell and you won't believe what happened next. She pulled down my trunks and I was the laughing stock of the crowd, but I must say the girls felt sorry for me they all wanted to go home with me, don't know what it was but from that day on I was the most popular boy of the gang, guess they liked what they saw.
Cheerios it's time to go, Jimmy

Folks can you kindly step aside this here message is for one very special lady and she knows who she is. Yes girl I got to come clean I'm a man of few words, I know you don't believe me, but what I am is a man of action so let me begin by saying girl, I do wanna get

next to you, till death do us part, let Rose Royce tell you some more, and know I love you more that life itself, bye bye, so long, Jimmy, sincerely yours
Rose Royce—I Wanna Get Next To You

Whenever I'm lost for words I ask myself what would Jesus say or do, than I get inspired and I write a revelation of my past experiences. So today I'm going to tell you the time I found a frog, not just any ordinary frog, this frog could jump like no other I have ever seen. Let me start from the beginning. I was driving down the road minding my own business when I see this frog and I immediately stopped the car and after 30 minutes I finally capture it and put it into a duffle bag to take home. Then it hit me I could make a killing if I enter it into the frog jumping contest at the state fair. When I got home I realized I had no place to put it so I filled up my Jacuzzi and threw the frog into the water. By this time I was full of mud so I jumped into the shower to rid me of all this mud that I had accumulated chasing the frog. Unbeknownst to me my girlfriend was bringing over four of her co-workers right after work to soak in the Jacuzzi. So they disrobe down to their birthday suits and hopped into the Jacuzzi. After about five ten minutes they started to feel something crawling onto their feet. So they each popped their heads into the water and before you can whistle Dixie they jumped out of the water screaming. So I run out of my tub naked like a jay bird to see what was going on. Low and behold there they were five naked women screaming their lungs out but before they could say a word I took my camera and took some photos. So when I explained that it was an authentic prize winning jumping jack frog that I was planning to enter in the ND State Fair in the jumping frog tournament in 10 months they settled down a bit but had to cover up so I wouldn't see their naked torsos or take any more photos. We later made a deal I would give them the photos if they would show me what they had, with no questions. Tonight it's Judy's turn, bye bye, Jimmy, aka the frog catcher
Leslie Gore—Judy's Turn To Cry

I was watching a Clint Eastwood movie, Josie 'Freaking' Wales or 'Hang 'em High' and I realized there's a lot of money to be made in the Bounty Business so I'm thinking that's what I want to do, chase mass murderers and bank robbers and score like a bandit. So I'm going to recruit some good men and women to join up. The good part it says wanted dead or alive, why waste the tax payers money we'll kill 'em, and then I put another notch on my lipstick case, I mean gun belt, I can see us now our photos taken over them dead bodies, we'll be famous and rich and let me warn you now if you've committed a heinous crime know you're on my hit list, ciao Jimmy . . .
Pat Benatar—Hit Me With Your Best Shot

Folks I want to go healthy this year so I got me a heifer of my own, yeah a cow, what else did you think I was referring to. So every morning at 4:30 like clockwork I'll run into my garage and milk Lucy. Yep, that's her name how did you know, my fortune teller told you, that gypsy woman can't keep a secret. My son said he would come over and help me, no way this aint going to turn out to be one of them there ménage a three; he just wants to squeeze her tits. Well them there tits are taken, nobody but nobody is going to squeeze her tits but me. Man oh man I get high just feeling them suckers, pardon the pun. Does anybody know how to turn that milk into butter or juicy fruit, well if you do, Gloria, kindly tell me the steps? Well got to go I think it's time for checking up on Lucy, hey mums the word

don't want everybody to know I got me a heifer, it's my business what I got and what I do all day, and I do it good, umm umm umm byeeeeeeee, Jimmy aka farmer Brown
Witness—Time For Milking

Can you keep a secret, I was breast fed till the age of 12, I guess that's why the attachment to them till this day. I'm what you call a born sucker. Hey, mums the word don't want people to know I'm a sucker but if you really must know they call me tucker cos I can also be a mother . . . . er, ciao got to go milk Sookie. Who's Sookie, that's my girl's name and you talk hugemongous, how does 41 24 39 sound to you, yep one hot hefer hahahaha byeeeeeeee Jimmy the all-day sucker, yeah I wish

As most of you don't know I am an entrepreneur waiting to happen and I just filed a patent for my latest invention, let me start from the beginning. When you go to the beach, lake, or a public pool what do you notice about the men. They are becoming top heavy; yeah I know it's not a pretty sight so I've invented a man bra. Don't laugh but it's true and I'm also developing a one piece bathing suit, yep just like the girls wear. Maybe even a two piece would be popular. I'm going to Brazil next week to try it out. Can you all see me now with a thong and a hooters bra? Yeah I'm starting to have breasts, and they are starting to sag. Hey please don't tell nobody cos I don't want anybody to steal my idea, but I have no fear I already filed a utility patent. Omg I'm going to look pretty when I hit the beaches, I'll be singing "I'm so pretty, very pretty". Might get sexy and daring and take it all off. Well over there it's the norm and I'll be frolicking on the beach and those girls will frolic with me. I might as well stay over there and ride on a float with all those naked girls when the Carnival comes into town. Oh you'll recognize me alrighty I'll be the one in all hot pink outfits, mask, thong, and my new invention, Jimmy's Man Bra jumping up and down. Hey if any of you want to join me, come along, and please bring your thongs and your skimpy bras. We'll be the drop dead gorgeous folks from da Eu Es of Aye. Now I know what they mean when a girl says to another girl "How's It Hanging," don't ask byeeeeeee,
Jimmy the inventor of the man bra

Folks can I tell you a story that happened to me just the other day, yep I'm the one, no really I'm the one who can predict the rain, tell your future, and do things to ya that will drive you up a wall. I can even raise the dead, last night I brought back this rooster to life, the owner was freaking pissed that critter woke them up for years so when it was poisoned they were jumping for joy until I arrived, enough of that. Call me next time you want me to perform a miracle and all this is because I'm the seventh son. Yep I got six other brothers and I will beat them silly if they give me the lip or the eye, don't effing mess with me. Enjoy Johnny Rivers; he too is the one, byeeeeeeeee, Jimmy
Johnny Rivers—Seventh Son

Does anybody know the meaning of diddy bop; well you are looking at the meanest and baddest diddy bopper that ever lived. When you roam the streets with a bunch of thugs notice how we walk. We sway our arms from side to side and with a dip in our hip almost like John Wayne, and when you see us coming you better step aside, maybe walk in the street or on the other side of the block cos we will kick your ass. Ok so I'm an ass kicker, but then nobody dare mess with me and get this when I'm alone I tend to run cos you never

know who would want to whip my behind. Shoo I knew when to diddy bop but never when I was alone, now that's the sign of a smart man, yeah I live to tell about it!!!!
Jimmy, the diddy bopper

When I was traveling abroad to the Netherlands, I made a big mistake I picked up a girl in an after-hours club and what I thought was going to be a friendly get together romp on the beach turned out I was her smorgasbord. She took me up to her place and wined me, and dined me, and in no time I was out of it, yep I was incoherent, naked, and famish like a horse. Don't need to tell you what she did to me, let's just say relationship between America and The Netherlands never been better we reached ecstasy. Can't tell you no more, a gentleman never tells. Well, let me end this with I wish you all a Merry Christmas and a Happy New Year, ta ta!!!

The following series of comments were posted directly into my Facebook Channel in a private group site called '**Did You Hear What Jimmy Said**.' I want to share with you some of my favorites and please note some of the names have been changed to protect the innocent. I hope you like them as much as I do, enjoy, Jimmy

Hey, can I tell you a true story; I met some of the nicest people on the face of the earth here at the Minot ING Service Center. Sometimes I didn't want to go home cos I couldn't get enough of them. I had three bosses while I was there, but it was a former Sargent, no names please, that really impressed me. She ran the department like a military tight knit unit. Sometimes I just wanted to get up and salute her. She would have made for a good drill instructor even though she was just a little gal. And I knew if you dared mess with her she would have taken you to the back and either pulled out a can of whip ass or shot you right there in the leg that you would then have walked or crawled a straight line no questions asked. I was sad to hear she was no longer in the center. Well wherever she went I know she is kicking ass, so let's all raise a glass to her, hip hip hooray, hip hip hooray. Thanks for your time and let's get together someday.

I want to take this time to dedicate this song to one of the members of the group in Facebook it's a no brainer whom I'm referring to but let's just say she is the bomb. When I worked with her at the ING Minot Service Center she always made my day and more so when her man would show up cos you talk crazy that man was crazy funny. Our boss, a former military Sargent, hated him cos whenever he mosied on in nothing got done, yep our productivity went from a stunning 110.99 to a measly 51.01. He made us laugh and cry at the same time. No I mean he was that funny. Now that I'm talking about him I got something in my eye and I'm not ashamed to say that, and in case you were not aware that man was a hero. I've had the privilege to know two heroes in my lifetime and he was just that, the genuine artifact. Didn't brag about it and I'm proud to say he was my friend, those of you who didn't know 'Big John' I can tell you this much you would have loved him. Thanks for listening me out and the next time you see Gloria tell her Jimmy says 'hey.'
Laura Branigan—Gloria

Folks in the above comment I was referring to a former co-worker of mine and her husband Big John Coyne, a war hero and a retired police officer. Sad to say we lost him a few years back and I will always remember him and my friend Gloria. And that former Sargent of ours liked big John and was deeply touched by his loss. Just wanted to clear that up, Thank you, Jimmy

When I worked at the Client Changes Department one of the functions we performed on a daily basis was making beneficiary changes. Sometimes a policy owner would request a change deleting a child/sibling probably out of a personal dispute for whatever reason. Then a short time later the owner would request another change adding that child/sibling back so he/she would be eligible for proceeds if the insured had died. Sometimes these types of changes would change over and over and over. Ours was not to question why but to do and die, pardon my pun. Also another change that we always found interesting was where one spouse would leave his or her spouse an article of clothing for example a leather jacket whatever. Why this request, we felt it was to put an end to a dispute should that jacket beneficiary would contest the distribution of the proceeds. This request let the courts know the owner was in clear mind when he/she omitted that person from getting any real monetary gain other than that article of clothing like a jacket. Well as I always say, something is better than nothing hahahahaha, thanks, Jimmy

Hey if any of you are still in touch with the Sarg, tell her I said 'hey' and that I miss her. She was da bomb, let me explain, when I would come into work late she would have me standing at attention and would preach the Army Book of Rules to me and after talking for a half an hour or so I would respond, "huh" and I could see she was going to burst a bubble so I throw her a wink and she excused me cos she thought that wink was a sign to meet me in the broom closet for lunch and that was without a sandwich. Well any way say 'hey' just the same, byeeeeeeeeeeeeee, Jimmy has spoken

Folks I got a story for you that you just aint going to believe heck I don't believe it myself. My friend who will remain anonymous, like hell she will, Peggy, her husband the big game hunter, aka Mr. Bowana J., the know it all, decides he wants to go lake fishing on New Year's Day cos he wants to start the new year on a bang. So he and his buddy bring along everything needed including lots of fishing gear, poles, lures, minnows, you know those little fish used to catch big fish. His favorite pink overall jumpsuit, big heavy duty boots and you just knew he was going to bring along his video camera and a still camera so he could capture the thrill of victory for posterity. Well after a few hours, 8 to be exact, all they were able to catch was a five gallon bucket full of fish barely enough to eat or stuff and mount on the walls. I think it's called taxidermy or some shit. Well after drinking their three cases of beer, Coronas, he only drinks the best, they cost five bucks a twelve pack they decide it's time to show off their bounty to the boys and wives back home, Peggy included. As they headed out of that frozen tundra they heard the sound of cracking, or was it popping, well they heard something and it didn't sound good. That's when his buddy, Lenny, lay back Lenny, had the brains to jump out of the vehicle and run for his dear life, smart guy. Now Mr. Bowana J, yeah Peggy's other half, can't say better half cos Peggy's got that title. He didn't have the nerve to abandon his prized possession, old Betsy. Yeah that's what he calls his 20 year old Toyota he had won in a card game the month before and before he could whistle Dixie his car goes down head first to the bottom of the lake with him in it. Eight feet down give or take a few inches, maybe four or five but who's counting. So he rolls

down his windows, smart move, and crawls out and floats to the top and hops on an iceberg that just happened to be floating by where he can now get on top and scream his lungs out for help. Now he can't use his spanking deluxe brand new phone cos it's all wet, good for nothing. At this point he is fuming mad crying his eyes out as to how he's going to get back to his lovely bride who has been watching cartoons and soaps all day long. She's a Looney Toons freak, and can't stop watching those soap opera programs now that Tad is cheating on Snookey from the Desperate House Wives, with that one who used to be called Lois Lane from Superman, you know the one. So he's mad as hell and wondering how he's going to get back home. So he cons a local farmer with a lure of a deer head, a possum and a squirrel to take him home without his buddy Lenny, who we later found out ran that ten mile stretch all the way home on his own. So Bowana J. arrives home late. Peggy is all cried out worrying when dinner was going to arrive and also cos her macho man has never been out this late before so she surmises he might have kicked the bucket. No that bucket had five gallons worth of fish that he took down with him and most likely got away. Talk about nine lives they got away with two but what do I know maybe they've been through this before and are working on lives three or four. Well the good news he made it out alive and the bad news he lost everything and as far as the car all they had on it was liability insurance and now its sitting at the bottom of the lake watching the fish that got away swim by. Sad to say Peggy had to have cereal for dinner, Fruit Loops, and the kids, tuna fish on a roll. I think we have the making for a Laurel and Hardy slapstick movie, where are they now when we need them and Peggy knowing her mentality is planning it and hoping to make a fortune, maybe with my help it's a done deal, 50 50, 25 for her and 75 for me, end of story, period.
Jimmy, the big story teller

Do you recall that story I told you about Peggy's husband, yeah Mr. Bowana J, well you aint heard the last of it. First of all let me describe what he looks like. He's a cross between John Wayne, Arnold Schwarzenegger, Rocky Balboa, and Ernest all rolled into one. One mean mother tucker with a vengeance machine. Well any way he took a liking to me cos he could see we were both suave and real macho men plus he heard of my reputation as a ladies man. So he invites me over to his log cabin house to show me all his trophies. That boy has all kinds of heads mounted on his walls, deer, antelope, possum, rabbits, squirrels and even a road hog and that's just in the first floor. He's got a bulls head, a full body spread of an eagle, a hawk, an anaconda and a queen bee, but there to the right was one big empty hole on the wall. So I say, I see one got away, and he gives me a dirty look, you know the kind, that can kill you in a heartbeat. So I say, just kidding and then he smiles. What you going to put there, then with a big ole grin, oh he has a beautiful grin even if I say so myself and no I'm not a fruit cake, I love women. So he says we're going to get it tonight and that's when he said I should come along. So in a manly voice in front of Peggy I said, OK!. That night he comes to pick me up, omg he was dressed to kill. He had guns and knives and machetes strapped all over his body even on his legs, arms and if that's not enough wearing his camouflage suit, hat included. All I had on was my low cut hip hugger Guess Jeans with the stars embroider every which way and my fruit of the looms boots, and my Levi jacket and Stetson hat I won in a poker game. So after driving 6 hours up north we finally arrive, and he tells me in a whisper we're there. So I say where is there, so he says Devils Ridge. So he parks his jeep and gathers his other weapons of mass destruction. His William Tell bow and arrow, his 30 yard six, Magnum 44, his Colt 45, and his grenade launcher. Me, all

I had was my 22 that comes in a 100% all leather casing. Here I'm thinking he's going for wild turkey or a goose. Had I known he was after bigger fish I might have stayed home and watched some Benny Hill or Mr. Bean or Debbie Does Dallas? So we trek up the mountain and after a half hour he informs me we're here for mountain lions or bears. That's all I had to hear, so I said I don't feel good I better go back down and rest and he gives me that dirty look again and watches me walk down. The next morning he shows up all beat up, shirt and pants all torn, bleeding like a pig, and dragging what appeared to me was a little ole teddy bear no more than 50 pounds. I was so glad he got what he wanted. Now on his wall is that mean ole little teddy bear. You should have heard him tell the story how he had to wrestle with it and was able to put a strangle hold on it for an hour before it succumbed, don't remind me. Now I know why Peggy fell for this big ole hunk of a man, he would have mounted her head on the wall had she refused his proposal of marriage? Poor Peggy she must have lived in fear all her life, but then again she was his biggest catch and she's worth more than all those other heads put together, end of story!!!!

Cyber Comedy,
The Jimmy And Marisol Story

Folks this is a riveting account of conversations between a man and a woman, he from the Eu Es of Aye and she from across the pond to the hills of Spain. They have never met and thank god they haven't because they are the funniest thing to come out since Lucy & Ricky, Sonny & Cher, Sally & Harry, or when Tom met Meg . . .

It's an international camaraderie between a man and woman. No this is not a romance story, nor a spy thriller; but do hold on to your hats just the same cos they will pick your pockets and you will want to give them all you have just to keep them telling you more and more. I guarantee one thing if nothing else, you will laugh and then some but don't take my word, read on!!!

Some think they are the reincarnation of Will & Grace, Ned & Stacey, Mork & Mindy, Sonny & Cher, Stiller & Meara, Lucy and Ricky, or Gracie and Allen but they sure know how to make you laugh without a script. His name is Jimmy, a shy quiet fellow who calls himself 'the boy from NYC,' struggling to make a living writing short stories and blogging on various cyber media web sites who's part time day job is working at a big retail store selling plumbing supplies, lumber and building materials, and telling jokes to anyone who will listen. And get this, the price is right, that's right, for free, nada, zilch, zero, so pull your hands out of your pockets and besides he's not allowed to take a tip. But he'll do lunch if you twist his arm and he loves Italian. Sometimes he gets a smile and sometimes a hearty laugh. Some even come back to hear more of his standup material that's why the big crowds in aisles six and seven at that building located at 73-01 somewhere in Queens but you didn't hear it from me.

Her name is Marisol who lives in Spain, a spit fire of a gal, pretty as a daisy to say the least who loves to entertain her friends and has become with no fault of her own the mother/house nanny to her family of four men, her father, and her three brothers. In her spare, whenever that is she like Jimmy posts videos and songs in her YT Channel where she can entertain all her many friends and anybody else who wants to listen.

The story you are about to hear is non-rehearsed, no scripts to follow, just comments back and forth to one another and the more they say the funnier it gets. Sometimes it is he who opens up with a crazy story and then she follows up with a reply that can be funnier than the opening comment. It's really a no win situation because at the end they end up praising one another and even that is funny. Hope it moves you and lets us realize that laughter indeed is a way to end all problems. Sit back and make yourself comfortable cos this will be one heck of a ride or call it what it is, a comedy sitcom in the internet, that's right through You Tube, you don't want to know, fuhgettabouditt . . . .

May 25, 2011 started out as a dismal quiet day and I was singing the blues, no not actually singing, just feeling a wee bit out of it and then out of nowhere appeared before my very own eyes this beautiful angel who uttered a big hello and before you knew it we were chatting constantly. It's as if the heavens opened up and the sun lit up the skies and a miracle occurred, it was so invigorating and I felt like a pig in slop, like a newborn sucking it's mother's breast, like a fish in water, like a load was lifted off my shoulders, it was so good to be alive. Well no need to tell you it was an omen, it was the first day I net Marisol, the second best thing that has ever happened to me here in 'You Tube.' What was the first, when I met Pookie Girl? Well it's been a blast, me and Marisol aka moorea2010 have been friends for what appears to me a lifetime. Enjoy this story, it's our story, and we want to share it with you, hope it moves you like it has us, enjoy, Jimmy and Chiquita Banana!!!!!

Marisol has subscribed to you on YouTube! (May 25, 2011)
Wow, what a nice comment you left on my channel Jimmy. I really appreciate it most of all the fact that we are gonna be friends from now on. Thanks for the invite and sub, I subbed back to your beautiful channel. I love the description you gave to some of your friends that is very nice of you :) . . . we have a common friend, Tricia
Please feel more than welcome to stop to say hello and share this new friendship between us . . . remember that my channel is your house 2 . . . . Have a great day and enjoy life 2 the max, because we live it only once :):) Greetings and hugs from Spain
M@risol

Thank you Marisol for your invite, it would be a pleasure and an honor to come over to your house, is eight o'clock too early for you. Yes in the morning, I do my best work when I'm bushy tailed and spunky. Living life to the max is my persona; to be honest I live life on the fast lane. Everything I do is spontaneous and that can get me into trouble. The last girl I went out with, her husband almost killed me, but let's not talk about this here it will only get me into more hot water. You did say you're single; well bless my soul I think we're going to be good friends after all, no let me correct that, best of friends . . . Ciao and how my lady,
Jimmy

Re: The Tango. So you are a writer, interesting, I will you for your books? What kind of writing do you do and don't tell me a good one,. mystery, fiction, drama, romance or history? Which one of them, or maybe one that I didn't mention?
M@risol

No, I don't use a translator, I learned English here and lived in USA for two years, so it's not perfect but I can survive. Here most of the people speak more than one language. You don't find many mono-lingual here unless are people who live in farms and things like that. The video 4 me was quite surprising. I didn't expect anything like it, but my friend was very nice and composed a song 4 me . . . yep . . .
I don't have bags around my eyes yet, hahaha and they are black . . . . even though the song says blue . . . I guess to match the rhyme :)
We'll talk tomorrow, byeeeeeeeee
The Divine Miss 'M', hahahaha, yes that's me, M@risol

Yes I'm a part time writer besides other things but within time you will get to know me inside out and hopefully we get acquainted. Maybe go out for a few drinks, take in a movie, I love the hot sexy adult kinky ones.
I used to be in a band, I played the drums, the organ, the symbols, the harp, and that big guitar looking instrument, you know that's bigger than a horse I think they call it a cello or a sumo guitar. I hate bragging but I've done it all. Btw can you sing, the reason I ask is because I can use a gal like you in a new band that I'm putting together and right after you sing I pass the hat around. I can see us now at the parks, in the bars, on the beaches, on the trains, in the rain, singing for money. And it's going to be 50 50 I most definitely insist, 75 for me and 25 for you, well I need to cover my expenses but don't worry you'll get your fair share. We'll be in the money and super rich. Got to go, working on a song, it's called Money, Money, Money.

Hahahahaha, why am I laughing cos I can't sing a lick to save my life but I'm a good hummer, that's what I do best? You see when you forget the lyric that's where I come in, I hum until you remember the words, see I'm good for something hahahaha . . . .
Ciao, Jimmy, your new partner in crime

Hahaha you are 2 funny Jimmy, I don't think we will survive singing. We'll be starving 2 death, hahaha. Maybe we have to look for something else. I don't know, how about some daredevil stunts I shoot you out of a cannon or you hold an apple in your teeth and I shoot it out of your mouth, hahahaha, just kidding. I'm glad you found me cos I don't recall seeing you before now, but hey it's never 2 late right, yeah :) and I'm happy 2 have you as a friend :):)
M@risol

Ok Marisol so singing is out of the question but would you be interested in being my lion tamer in a circus act. You see I'll be on the outside of the cage as you go in to whip the eight lions into shape, but one false move and I'll shoot the lions, all of them if I have to. So you'll be alright, hey a little chewing won't kill ya hahahaha. Well got to get going to pick an outfit for you, hmmmm a two piece or a one piece, decisions, decisions, decisions. Now you know why I get 65 and top billing and you 35 and low billing, cos I'm the brains of the outfit, ciao Jimmy the Lion Tamer & Co, that's you, Co, short for company . . . .

Hey Marisol, I don't know if I told you about me being a male model besides a bunch of other things. Well I was hired as a model for this art school and you can't imagine how many women are into the arts and figure painting, there are twenty girls to every one guy and when I go in to pose down to my shorts they draw me. See I get paid to model in the nude except the total buff part occurs at the end and that's when I up the modeling price to 150 dollars an hour and that's from every student there, yaaaah hooooo. I go home with a pocketful of spending loot, don't ask. When the professor asks me to disrobe, meaning take my shorts off, I get a bit jittery and nervous but what the heck and you should see the faces on them there girls and the professor, she has to sit down or she'll faint. I was what they say in the horse racing business "in the money" or as they say "hung like a blue ribbon." Oh well, enjoy the video and yes I am for hire if you want me, we can do it in one of two ways, in private or in public, but you got to pay me if you want some of this, hahahahaha. Ciao Jimmy, Boy Atlas, hahahahaha yeah that's what they call me besides other things, you don't want to know!!!

Ps
The only house rules: no cameras or touching allowed, now in private that's another story, there are no house rules, but then I charge for the extras, ooooooo weeeeee, good god, more money . . . .
Male Model—Man Posing Nude For Art Class f/k/a Male Model gets excited

Jajaja, yep, I have seen this video before and is a total laugh all the way. When those marbles jump in the air is hilarious and his face is like a poem trying to keep a straight face, it doesn't matter how many times I see it I always laugh 2 the extreme. $150 bucks, you mean cash, it could be cheaper if you came by me cos if I exchange for Euros it will be less than that, hahaha. U are crazy, I think you are the one who have some. ummmm special strong beverage from the Witch Doctor that makes you insane . . . jajaja . . . . We are quite a pair, at least funny, don't you think? Leo/Aquarius, it'll be a lot of roaring and swimming, haha . . . :):) I wish you a good night and lovely dreams with angels included for the price of one, jajaja, byeeeeee
M@risol

Jajajaja . . . . I'm gonna have the best YT partner in the world . . . 65/15 . . . . Ummmmm let me think about it . . . jajaja . . . . U are 2 much 2 . . . I think that we match very evenly on that respect . . . jaja . . . I'm glad I don't make you cry. It could be worse; at least I make you laugh a little, love a little, and live a little . . . Ummm probably you are gonna get more of my funny quotes 4 your book I'm sure about that . . . I know a lot of jokes but in Spanish . . . but when you translate it, you miss a lot of the flavor and funny parts . . . byeeeeeeeeeee,
The Divine Miss 'M'

Well you can say all the jokes you want cos this is the stage where you can open up and show the world what you've really got, no not that, your gorgeous mind. Hey don't be getting crazy on me now, we're writing a book and everybody is gonna know your name. Btw what is your nick name everybody's got a nickname, some call me big boy, some killer and you can call me anything you want but never late for rehearsal hahaha. I bet I fooled you, you thought I was gonna say dinner, no that's been said and done for ages, we're a new breed, all our phrases and jokes will be original and yes everybody will know our name, Jimmy and Marisol, the hunk and the hottie. Hey, get to sleep we got practice tomorrow, c ya then,

Jimmy

U are quite an interesting person with a lot of experience and good PSICOLOGY about people 2 . . . I'm I right?

OMG Jimmy you are gonna kill me laughing, would you like the high heels I have on my BG, they are sexier than boots, siiiiiihhhhhhhh. I won't say to anyone . . . . U are so funnnyyyyy . . . I can't stop laughing with your post. My muscles from the stomach hurt cos I laugh for over 5 minutes . . . . like those u try to stop, but keep laughing even harder It was like that, I don't know if I can survive, hahahaha . . . I love it and please get out of the closet, my closet, taking my high heels . . . . hahaha . . . is not what you think sweetie . . . hihihi

I'm glad I make smile instead of cry that would be horrible. U are right, I'm extremely outgoing and social 2 the max, that is my personality. I'm a Leo all the way, what sign are you!!!

The Divine Miss 'M'

Marisol if you must know I'm Aquarius and proud of it, my fortune teller told me I was a one of a kind, a rare specimen and I must agree cos I read my own fortune from that crystal ball you gave me and I was sitting on a throne, no not that one in the bathroom, you silly goose, in a castle of some kind surrounded by my loyal subjects. You were sitting to the right of me hahaha. See I told you you'd be coming with me. I love it when you entertain me with your belly dance routine oooooo weeeeee. Well I gotta go, she's gonna flip the tarot cards next and tell me some more, bye bye my dancing queen . . .

J

Re: They Think I'm Crazy ahhhhhahahajajaja . . . . What do you have in your medicine cabinet Jimmy, a rainbow of pills? Viagra 2 ??? Hahahaha, this is 2 much, U want 2 kill me laughing here. Let me tell you, your wife or girlfriend they will never get bored with you, it's nonstop comedy, no wonder your books are like that . . . . your humor is hilarious, my god!!!!!!!

Having a friend like you is a blessing and I feel blessed with your friendship . . . Thanks 4 these moments of happiness and good camaraderie it's out of this world. Are you sure you are from this planet??? Is unreal :) . . . hahaha I'm very happy that we came across in this virtual world and be good friends now. It is funny after few messages sent I feel like I know you 4 quite a awhile. Chemistry my friend that's what it's all about among people, sometimes you make the right connection, sometimes you don't :(

M@risol

Oh I've known you way before we met, just couldn't pinpoint who you were till that angel told me of your coming, so yes I feel like we're the best of friends, destiny couldn't keep us apart no how, love you crazy woman . . . . Jimmy

Marisol I hate to boast, what does boast mean, that's when I walk the walkway and show it off, now back to my story, back in the day I was known as 'The Hustler,' why you ask, I could single-handedly dance up a storm with not 1, not 2, or 3, but 4 girls and you are looking at them. Btw try not to interrupt me when I'm telling you a story. Heck, I taught those girls everything they know and then some but I rather not go there, I was a little drunk and didn't know what I was doing but they say I was doing it good and fellas you would be proud of my exploits. So sit back and watch my girls work, you don't see me, but I'm in the front, all dressed up like Jimmy Travolta strutting my stuff. What now, what is strutting, walking cocky with a dip in your hip and like doing the runway bad as can be, nobody want to f%3k with you!!!

Pans People—The Hustle

Do The Hustle . . . jajajajaja, I can see you are a handful sweetie . . . Ummm so I have to be good in order 2 get some tango lessons from you, as you know tango is a very sensual dance so it's not easy dear, jajajajajaja . . . U crack me up I can't believe that in only a few messages we feel like we know each other, is that chemistry? I'm not talking about a lab, jajaja, oh well!!!! I can teach you some flamenco but you have 2 be good 2. I will send you a video from one of the best flamenco dancers we have here; on top of that he's saxy to the max, one of a kind. Let me find the video, I hope you like it, not him, the video, hahahaha . . . insane . . . Let me find it 4 you. Did you see the video on my feature? A friend composed a song 4 me yesterday. It's awesome :):):)

By the way sweet dreams again and again for my new relative: D Byeeee

Marisol I don't know about sensual but is the Flamenco something like the Mexican Hat Dance cos I can see me trying to do it after having a few drinks. By then I don't care how I look just as long as I'm having a good time and people throw money my way into the hat once I flip it over. You probably think all I'm interested is money. No, that's not what I'm about but I do consider it a bonus for my efforts and for making a fool of myself. What I'm really interested is having a good time and that I please the lady that I'm with. I'm a lady pleaser and some would say a lady killer first, then an entrepreneur second. So do you have a money maker of your own, you know, do something for the folks to throw some money your way. You told me we would starve if we were to sing as a duo and that scared the heck out of me cos it was you who I was counting on to support us. Well you did say you're a terrific dancer then I bet you can you do a belly dance or something along those lines hahahaha, I won't ask. Well we better get you trained cos I like living the vida loca, loco same shit, good life, and that means we need money, money, and more money. Well partner it's time to say adios and vaya con dios and yes god help us . . . .

Jimmy, your better half to be, your partner in crime

Hey, can you at least drive a getaway car; I got a plan 'B.'

OMG . . . you are way 2 funny Jimmy!!!! hahaha, so now I'm your sister, the only problem I'm not a Correa :) . . . how about a friend??? Correa is a well-known last name here, so you have some Hispanic blood in your veins. Interesting my friend and on top of that you dance merengue, tango, and more . . . quite a dancer my new friend . . . Let me tell you, I'm a good dancer myself since I was little and I know how 2 dance those rhythms and I love them. By the way tango is the only one that I don't know, it's 2 difficult to dance. You have to be Argentinian to do it or get some ballroom dance lessons, hahaha. I will teach you some flamenco, how about that? I'm happy that you are such an outgoing and friendly person, that's good, we'll get along well cos I'm like that 2, hahaha. Have a gr8 night and

sweet dreams and remember to smile always, it causes a good impression on others and its free 2, hahaha. :):):):D Hugs from a distance . . . .
M@risol.

Thank god we're not related cos then I couldn't tell you sweet nothings and you are so damn saxy and downright funny. Yes we are both outgoing and friendly and I would love to spend many a night with you, getting to know you, your likes, your dislikes, and what turns you on. Then I would work my sweet charms and give you what you like, all of me, hahahaha.
Bye bye Sweet Pie, and do enjoy Julio and Miss Ross with "All of You" or is it All of Me, you choose whatever floats your boat . . .
Jimmy

Marisol I got a story you're not going to believe and you better tie a knot on your bloomers cos what I am about to tell you will blow them away. l once looked a lot like Elvis, heck I even imitated him right down to the voice, here check this out, "A HUCKA, HUCKA BURNING LOVE, I SAID A HUCKA, HUCKA BURNING LOVE" yep that was me singing but any way back to my story, when you do a lot of drugs, sex, and rock and roll, see what can happen to you. It's like a fountain of youth; I look like a kid, thank you. Yes that's me alright and the girls all love me. Heck Elvis would have been proud of me. Well stay tuned cos I got a lot more of Elvis imitations in me yet, like when I swivel my hips or pucker my upper lip, hot dog or is it hound dog. Oh Yeah, Jimmy, the new King of Rock 'N Roll!!!

Gipsy reporting live from Gipsy Camp in Rumania, well sweetie I see you are Elvis re-incarnated, the hair is the same but the difference is that you 'sticked' your finger in the electric outlet and VOALAAAAAA . . . instant SPIKES, hahaha!!!!! Always a treat to see you and have that good laugh that only you can provoke in me every time I read your crazy messages, hahaha. I love you my friend and please never change otherwise POOKIE won't pay attention 2 you. And by all means keep the windows wide open for tonight's show; we'll call it an encore, maybe standing room only, ajajajajajaja :): D
Much love, kisses and good vibes and the Gipsy Good Luck included 4 free 4 you, no 65/35 . . .
besitos
T.G.I.F . . . Gipsy Queen

Marisol now I know why you are so popular, you have the knack for picking the right songs and they are all so entertaining and so diversified, an instrumental one day, a tango or some other dance song another day, you mix it up with Spanish and English songs. And you don't stop there, a French tune, a Portuguese song so it does prove your channel is all that and a bag of chips. I can see how and why you have so many friends and why everybody, males and females alike, want to be your friend. I'm so glad I became one too . . . ciao,
Jimmy, aka Sherlock 'Elementary' Holmes

Your comment was awesome sweetie. I really appreciate it from the bottom of my heart. I'm glad you like it and you know me, I don't like to be boxed in the same kind of music,

it's too boring 4 me. I like to surprise my friends with different things and don't make my channel predictable for everybody. I like the surprise factor, hahaha :):) . . . . Btw how is Pookie, 'Living La Vida Loca' with you, hahaha. I love your featured video is totally hilarious, hahaha. Well sweetie have a lovely night and sweet dreams, tomorrow I will come back with one of my crazy stuff . . . . let me get the inspiration . . . hahaha, much love and kisses . . .
M@risol

Well Marisol that's what separates me from the rest of the pack, I'm a born leader, people follow me every which way I go especially the womenfolk I'm not a one hit wonder kind of guy. Once you get to know me and me of you I like to tell you sweet things and maybe we hook up. You did say you're not married well neither am I, and Pookie, well she's just a friend we go out and party but I am a single man and can change my mind any time I want. Btw I only date ladies who are willing and able. Heck we can sneak off into the night, you know like on a secret lover's rendezvous. I will more than thrill you. Did I tell you I'm a hunk and I can seduce any woman I see and want? You might be in luck; I'm free on Fridays, Mondays, and Tuesdays. Well call me if you should ever want to meet and talk, I'll talk your ears off hahaha and shake your tree and I hope you like Steve Miller Band, I taught him all he knows and that's how he got to write that song, "The Joker," and his first name isn't Maurice . . . . Ciao, Jimmy
Steve Miller Band—The Joker

Hey Lover Boy, I got some exciting news Ummmm, you were my 29 thousand,100th commenter on mi channel so you win a crystal ball, hahahaha now you and Pookie can start your own fortune telling business. You know where you read palms, flip tarot cards, and look into the future of your customers and reveal their destinies, hahaha. I know, I know, what are friends for, you don't have to thank me, and besides I love you like almost family, where did you say you come from, hahahaha . . . only kidding, love you big time,
M@risol

Marisol I like it when you call me lover boy and for your information with that crystal ball I can make a lot of money, open up a store front and lure in all the ladies with promises of eternal life and a whole lot of love. What happens next, que se yo, but maybe I put on a porno movie and tell them if they want to be a star in my show I can make it happen. How's that, I get them good and drunk and once they are out cold take photos of me and them in our birthday suits and when they come too I show them the photos and that will prove I gave them what they wanted, me, hahahaha. And then I tell them if they want more, me that is, bring money and more money . . .
Ciao, here comes one now, got to go, got to go, enjoy Led Zeppelin with "Whole Lotta Love" . . .
Jimmy, the love man but you already know that
Led Zeppelin—Whole Lotta Love

Jimmy I just knew you would make good use of that crystal ball and make all the ladies happy and I'm happy 4 you 2 . . .
Mar y sol

Marisol I looked into that crystal ball yesterday, yes the one you sent me and I noticed it was made in China. Girl you could have sent me an original gypsy artifact made by one of your relatives, aunts, uncles, cousins, brothers, or sisters cos I hear you come from a long line of gypsies. I won't tell you who told me, that's a secret and heck you and Pookie might be related by a great great, great, great gypsy king or something and do you know what that would make us, family, hahahaha. Well, any way I see that you will become rich and famous, a world renowned party planner. You'll be mingling with the Iglesias, no not the church Iglesias, Julio, Enrique, and Jr. Iglesias, and J. Lo, Marc Anthony, Shakira, Tina, Celine, and Elvis. No not that Elvis, Elvis Costello Elvis, hahaha. I see you still not too bright, not working with a full deck but you'll be rich just the same. And me, poor as ever with a worthless ball made in China. Hey, no more gifts please, you showed me your true colors, cheap, cheap, cheap, bye bye, bye, bye Jimmy

Hey Pookie-Mon I already talk to my cousin, first blood gipsy, and he's gonna make a new 'Made In Spain' crystal ball with SPECIAL POWERS just 4 you, hahaha. U will see, your success is gonna spread like poison ivory or ivy, I don't know how they call it in your neck of the woods, like wildfire is more like it. Heck everybody in Nueva York will know your name and will go see you. Forget about the night clubs and strip houses. Ummmm, is gonna be Jimmy, The Fortune Teller. I will be your first customer and for FREE, not your 65/35 split that gets me even less, no way Jose . . . . hahaha. This gipsy is signing out for the night. Sweet dreams my friend and lots of kississsss 4 you . . .
M@risol

Pookie-Mon, hahahaha you're so funny already you make a game out of me. Well it better be the genuine thing this time cos if it aint I'm going to crack that ball into a million little pieces. Special powers, what's that, can it predict rain or a blizzard or if the price of gold is going up. Hey I don't need to know if the price is going up, it's how am I going to get me some money to buy some; and about the rain and blizzard, I just poke my head out the window and I can tell you just that, no I'm not a brain surgeon just one smart cookie, and I like to have my cake and eat it too, ciaooooo Missy,
Jimmy, Mr. Know It All and then some . . . .

Surprise, surprise, surprise, the gipsy friend is back with your authentic crystal ball made in Spain for you. My cousin (pure gipsy blood) made it especially 4 you. So you better take a good care of it, it's my present 4 you and remember when you become super famous in NY never forget who give it 2 you, me :):) . . . Sweet dreams my friend and have a wonderful night filled with kisses and dancing senoritas jajajaja!!!
M@risol

Marisol I got some good news and I got some bad news, so what do you want to hear first. Ok the good news. I'm in the money; my cash register is filled to the brim that I had to stick some in my socks. The ladies are coming in by the droves or as you would say dozens, the bad news; I can't keep up with them. Making love all day and all night has me exhausted, I got no time for myself. I like watching cartoons, Bugs Bunny, Popeye, Daffy Duck and all those Westerns, now I can't enjoy even that. And what's worse, I haven't slept in two days and I'm starting to look like a prune with all those bubble baths that I'm taking.

And if Pookie finds out you can fuhgettaboudit, she'll cut my . . . . Well no need to esplane but let's just say my voice will turn out to be more like Pee Wee Herman, than John Wayne my hero. So tell me what I should do, hey, what am I talking about you're the one that got me into this mess by sending me that new authentic crystal ball. I'm going to send it back and you can put it where it don't shine, need I draw you a picture, hahahaha byeeeee
Jimmy

Hahaha, you are crazy my sweet friend. I told you that crystal ball will be your lucky one cos it was sent by me. The Lucky Gipsy :):) . . . . I bring luck to people, did you know that? Now you are so busy I see you can't even keep up with your ladies, poor you . . . . Do I have 2 send you 2 a resort in the Caribbean and rest 4 a week? I think it will be a good idea and please take POOKIE otherwise she will be mad as h . . . with you, don't be the next Robert Bobbitt . . . hahaha. Ohhhhh well, just hide all the knives and scissors just in case. That's all folks, Looney Toones saying good bye . . . . farewell . . . so long . . . . hasta la vista baby.
Besitos and take care, hey I'm going on vacation next week to the Caribbean but not with you and Pookie :)
T.G.I.F . . . Gipsy Queen :) . . .

You're Looney alright and I can see I'll be home while you'll be having a good time in the Caribbean drinking piña coladas and doing god only knows what without me, oooooooohh I'm so mad, call me when you return we got business to discuss. And enjoy the song by Rupert Holmes "Escape, (The Piña Colada Song)" he too spends his time at the beaches drinking piña coladas in the buff; don't ask ajajajajaja, I'm starting to sound like you more and more each day
Jimmy

Re: I just wanna spend my life with you Yessssssssssss. I know what; you will be the next Lorena Bobbit case 4 sure . . . . Do you have woods behind your house? If it's an apartment lock the trash cans, hahahaha. Where is the magnifier? Omg you are gonna kill me . . . But I can't resist 2 tell you that U are too funny and a good friend. That's why I wrote 2 you share the "MARACAS" . . . A Little Bit . . . hahahaha.
I won't change sweetie, I will be the same until the day I die, its sounds like a song hahaha . . .
ta ta, M@risol

Marisol, Marisol, Marisol what am I going to do with you. You want to cut me up and no less my you know what. Well I'm in The Guinness Book of Records and it's a monument and besides my family jewels needs it too, so stop thinking like that and please don't ever mention that Lorena girl ever again, ouch hahahaha.
Jimmy

Marisol congratulations you are my one thousand, six hundred and ninetieth commenter on my channel so you just won an all paid expense trip for ten to NOWHERE. Yes and you and your guests can leave and return any time you so desire and spend as much as you want or got. Wow you are lucky, so please choose wisely and don't be late hahahahaha. Why am I laughing, cos this is the first prize anybody has ever won on my channel? Ciao and enjoy

your trip, bye bye, farewell and here's your hat, what's your hurry. Don't worry you can thank me later, oh much later there's no hurry, byeeeeeeeeeee
Jimmy
Btw, I'm thinking of changing my name from 'the artist formerly known as theloveman11378' to just 'J,' so call me 'J,' c ya later gator!!!

I am thrilled and jumping for joy with that trip to NOWHERE I won in your channel Jimmy excuse me 'J', hahaha, so where am I going? Let me guess, NOWHERE!!! hahaha. At least in my channel you won a crystal ball something you can feel and touch. So now you and sweet Pookie can become fortune tellers, hahaha . . . . I want you 2 read my palms and tell me my FANTASTICO future, I hope it's good; if not I won't pay you Mr. Gipsy Man not even give you a tip. But I do want you to have a great night and have all the fun you deserve with POOKIE-LiCIOUS, okay? Hundreds of kississsssss and huggiessss . . . . hahaha
M@risol

Marisol it's funny you should say but me and Pookie-Licious take a bubble bath before and after, before and after what, girl you still aint too bright, let me explain. When we are in the mood all she has to do is wink her eye and I run into the bath tub and filler up with Champagne, exotic oils, and we hop in and we give each other a good scrubbing and . . ., and . . . . , well I can't say it here cos all our friends will know, but then we hop into bed and wooooo it's bliss heaven. And after a few hours, 3 or 4 of nonstop caressing and probing, hahaha, I like to probe, don't ask, we hop back into the bubble bath and if we get thirsty drink some of that Champagne we poured into the water hahahaha, you don't want to know what happens next, we make love in the tub, rub a dub tub shhhhh, gotta go Pookie she's a calling me, bye
J, the artist formerly known as the love man

Marisol, I'm a certified genuine dirty dancer, let me explain. Back in the day I auditioned for that movie "Dirty Dancing" and did not get the lead part, Patrick something or other Swayze, that cheating dog got the part cos he was messing around with the producer's wife and she got him the part. Me, I was just an extra but I did dance in the movie, don't tell no one cos I feel bad I didn't get the lead but I know my time is yet to come. I will win Oscars, and Tony's, and Billboards, and every award you can think of. And when I make it big I'll let you be one of my girls hahahaha ok, ok, my main squeeze are you happy hahahaha, bye bye love ya . . . .
J

U got Patrick part 2, hahaha, your main squeeze? Do you think I am an orange and you can make orange juice with me, jajajaja just kidding, I know what you mean hahaha. Btw is there a full moon out tonight by any chance? auuuuuuuuuu¬auuUUUU . . . . Jimmy you are 2 funny and every message from you is refreshing and bubbling like champagne or maybe a bubble bath, hahaha, you pick which one is better 4 you . . . . Bubbleliciousssssss . . . . ahahahahahahahahahahaha
M@risol

Marisol that's my gypsy woman, yes the one with all those sweet charms and lovely brown eyes who hypnotizes me with love and sorcery. My, my can she dance and when our eyes meet ooooooooooo weeeeeeeeee that is all we need cos she drives me wild with passion and I go bonkers. What's bonkers, I eat it up hahaha. And when she whispers in my ears it is then that I know I have to have her all for myself. They say she was an offspring of a European nobleman, from the UK somewhere, I don't know where exactly maybe Jamaica, Australia, Scotland, Ireland, or was it Wales and her mother was a nomad gypsy queen who had all the men fighting for her hand. Well tonight I become the victor taking her to my home where I try every which way to seduce her but it will be I who will be seduced. We will make love for hours on end and we will hold each other all through the night. When I awaken she will have prepared a feast for me and we have it in bed hahaha yep in bed say no more. That gypsy woman if you all must know is my Pookie Girl and I love her to death . . .
Ciao J, the artist formerly known as the love man
The Impressions—Gypsy Woman (1961)

Ahaaaaaaaaaa I see your gipsy girl is no other than Pookieeee Girl hahaha. I don't have to be a mind reader or have a crystal ball in front of me to figure that out. I'm telling you that Pookie is the luckiest girt in the world because having a?????, how can I say it, an unspectant guy like you is always a thrill hahaha. Well I brought some jewelry for Pookie as a gift; maybe she will like it and wear it tonight for you when she dances the 7 Vails Dance 4 you, hahaha . . . I better go before I start teasing you. U don't want a nightmare tonight, just your POOKIEEE HOOKIEEEEE GIRL, hahaha
Kisses & huggies from this Gipsy Queen . . . . no land of confusion . . . haha :D::D:D:D:D . . .
T.G.I.F.

Hahahaha, what the heck is "unspectant" is that some kind of disease cos I surely aint got it, heck I can't even pronounce it, you sure are one smarty pants!!!
J

Hahahahaha, now I've seen it all, bull fighters, merengue dancers, pole dancers, but a singing clown, now that's too much to handle. Tell me Marisol you're not back on that Puerto Rican Bacardi Rum again are you, hahahaha. Last time you were, you told me you could walk on water and dance like Fred Astaire or was it Ginger Rogers. Well I thought your stay at the funny farm, you know that crazy asylum, had cured you for good, heck you were making beautiful weaving baskets and even though your pottery had too many holes in it, it was good therapy just the same but I can see you've flipped your wig again. Don't worry this time they'll give you electric shock treatments you will die for hahahaha, bye bye and please be good for something or else . . .
J, aka Doctor Feel Good

Jogglinnngggg . . . . joggglingggg, the clown is here, hahahahaha. U made me laugh so hard with your comment on my beautiful song. U have to understand it's a very powerful and sentimental song that touches your heart. I get goose bumps every time I listen to it. I wish he has an English version of it . . . .
M@risol

Marisol that's Smokey Robinson still cruising after all these years singing "Crusin" that would be a top # four hit in 1980. Well it's true what he's saying cos once Pookie and I get together it's a nonstop trip cos all I want to do is to be with her and nothing can pry us apart. Last night we made love and put on a show for our neighbors who thought I didn't know they were peeping through our bedroom windows. So I got into my birthday suit hahaha, yes buck naked, and rattled them and whatever else needed rattling hahaha and it was nonstop love from start to finish. I even threw in a few hoots and hollers and after an hour or so I got up and mooned them. This morning I bumped into them in the street and asked them how they liked my performance and they pretended they knew nothing of it. Tonight I will set up the trampoline and shake it up a bit letting it all hang out with our bits going every which way. Enjoy Crusin,
ciao, J, the artist formerly known as the love man
Smokey Robinson—Crusin

Helloooooo Mr. Gipsy friend, do I have to send you an invite and a Limo and put out a red carpet 4 you Majesty in order to visit me, hahaha, just kidding sweetie. I just want to pull your legs a little bit. I hope you had a gr8 weekend and the new week is full of good and magic 4 you. I always miss a good friend like you, but that's ok, your busy life won't let you socialize, hahaha . . . Miss Chiquita Banana is out and about, ciaooooo ciaooooo bambinooo . . . . baci, baci, baci :D T.G.I.F . . . .

Ahahahaha so now you're Miss Chiquita Banana, I didn't know Spain was an exporter of fruits and bananas no less. I love bananas, I eat one every day, taste so yummy and it's a good source of protein or plutonium, well something that's for sure. No I wasn't avoiding you just busy practicing my John Wayne walk and talk, see over here if you carry a big stick and look tall on the saddle nobody will mess with you and it usually works. Well when it doesn't work I run, and I do run like a rabbit, hahahaha. You see like Clint Eastwood, another of my heroes, you got to know your limits and I know when the odds are against me to hightail it out of there. That's why I live to tell another story. Well good night sweetie it was nice chatting with you. It's always a pleasure chatting, I learn a lot from you. Chiquita Banana that's what you are, hahahahaha you sure are fruity if ever there was one, you most definitely take the cake and eat it too hahahaha . . ., so long, hasta la vista
Arnold, I mean J . . .

Wooooooow, Pookie must be in heaven after this beautiful and meaningful words you left 4 her. What a big man you are, and how lucky she is, hahaha. You are One In A Million you . . . Is like hitting the big lotto jackpot, ummmm, priceless I guess hahaha. I want a ticket, hahaha :):)
Well changing da subject, thanks sweetie for your sweetness and fantastic friendship with me. I feel more than blessed 2 have such a, a, . . . ummmm??? amazing friend like you :) I don't have 2 tell you, endless kisses, love and smiles 4 you, and say hello to Pookie
M@risol

Yes I'm big and big all over, you don't want to know, and you can ask Pookie if you really must know. I don't like to brag, but that's why I'm in the Guinness Record Book, pages 131, 589 and 892 paragraphs 3, 4 and 5, 1, 2, and 3 through 6; but don't just take my word, see the photos, and believe me that's me, they don't show my face cos I told them not too. Omg if they had all the women would be all over me, following me like jack rabbits, hahahaha.

Thank you Marisol for your lovely compliments, not everyone can be amazing, heck I amaze myself sometimes the way I carry myself, I can be gentle like a pussy cat or ferocious like a rattle snake, no correct that, an anaconda. I can swallow you up; don't test me cos I'll eat you up in no time. hahahaha ciao and how,
J, the artist formerly known as the love man

Where are you my friend? Let me guess, the Chippendale hired you and one of those crazy ladies kidnapped you. Poor Pookie she must be going nuts, hahaha. Seriously, I worry about you Jimmy. I want my close friends, close, and I didn't see you the entire day yesterday and nothing today. What happened, please my friend as soon as you can give me a signal and tell me you are ok Pleaseeee . . . Much love, caring and kisses . . .
M@risol

Hey it's funny you should say that, I once tried out for Chippendales and I was disqualified cos the guys got together and threatened to quit if I were picked. You see I am too much, well not me, it was what I had to offer and the girls would go bananas over what I have, pardon the pun, hahahaha. Hey that sounds familiar weren't we discussing bananas a few days ago, oh well let's change the subject, I'm just too much. Hey you know anybody looking for a hunk with the most. Who am I talking about, me, girl get with the program it's all me 100% all beef and solid as a rock. Well call me if you think you can handle the kid, bye bye gorgeous, love to love you, Jimmy, and do enjoy Ashford and Simpson, "Solid as a Rock," that's me all the way . . . .

Ps
Oh, you are so sweet always worrying about me, well I do have to work and sometimes I come home all beat up, no not like I was attacked, beat up, like tired beat up. Sorry if I made you worry, well try not to I'm a big boy and I can take care of myself byeeeeeeee
Ashford and Simpson—Solid As a Rock

Marisol I got a secret to tell you, I bought one of them there pottery making whatcha ma call it thingy cos I want to surprise Pookie with it. I'm going to give it to her, no not that, but yes I'm working on that too that's the purpose of all this hahahaha. And I will try to reenact this scene from the movie 'Ghosts.' When she doesn't expect it, I come from behind and sit there with her and as she's making pottery I gently kiss her from behind, starting from her neck and working my way to her ear. Nibble it a bit, what is nibble, when you bite it gently ohhhh that will drive her wild, I hear some women have a G-Spot there. What's a G-Spot, who knows I think it curls her toes and makes the hair on her neck stand up and then she goes berserk? Oh man I can't wait, tell you about it tomorrow . . . Signing out from Never Never Land,
J
The Righteous Brothers—Unchained Melody (Ghosts)

Marisol I got some good news and some bad news. Pookie and I tried that reenactment of that love scene from "Ghosts" but when she jumped up to wrap her legs around my thighs we fell to the ground and bumped heads but that didn't stop me as I was bleeding with 'cichones'(bumps) and bruises we sailed on through and I must tell you, I was Captain of the Ship, Errol Flynn, would have been proud of me as we sailed the high seas hahahaha, if you get my drift. The bad news we had clay all over us and we had to take a long hot shower but then the good news, it was one hot shower to die for hahaha, ciao,
J
The Righteous Brothers—Unchained Melody (Ghosts)

Ummmm is a little risky making a pottery piece with you. I feel sorry for Pookie, hahahahahaha is gonna be a Masterpiece perfect for the Louvre Museum in Paris . . . . have you think about that? U will be the competition 4 the Mona Lisa, poor Da Vinci, he's gonna die again, hahaha!!!!!!!! Ohhhhh well, we'll see after you have finished with thatttttt. I better go before I get in deep water here, there is no lifeguard and I don't know how 2 swim, hahaha, just kiddin'. I'm like a fish, a mermaid, the little mermaid at that, oppppssss good byeeeeeee and pottery kisses . . . terracotta color :):) T.G.I.F . . . . hahaha
M@risol

Hahahaha it seems I always try too hard or maybe I get so excited and the beast in me comes out. Heck I was only trying to make some good pottery that's why the hands on but then we got carried away, our juices were over flowing and before you knew it, para bing, para bang . . . Hey, who the heck is DaVinci, and why didn't you tell me you were going to the beach, oh well hope you had a good time and you didn't over do yourself. Bet you must be smoking hot all over hahaha, no not what you're thinking hahahaha. Bye bye Gator, after while crockadile,
J, the artist formerly known as the love man

My best advice 2 you . . . . open a POTTERY SCHOOL . . . . U will have Pookies from left 2 right . . . . hahaha :):) . . . oppppppppssssssssss¬ :):)
M@risol

I'm sure after the pottery class U got the, ROL, Roll Dick Rollll . . . . ajajajajaja and puleesee don't get electrocuted you'll go up in smoke ajajajajaja . . .
The Divine Miss M

Funny, funny, funny, see you're at it again with me getting electrocuted, why always all the bad things have to happen to me, why can't it be you electrocuted that would be funny and your hair up instead of down hahahahaha, I can see it now ahahahaha
J

This is not the Titanic . . . . I'm not Rose, Mollie Brown, or Pookie either . . . . hahaha . . . . kisses and much love on the way 4 you Pott-ery friend :)
M@risol

Wow that was so nice of you to send me off on my journey, where am I going to, don't tell me, to Nowhere!!!!, you've been there and done that hahahaha.
Love you, Jelly Bean,
J

Helloooooo Mr. Pott-ery . . . hahaha . . . ummm sure you though that I forgot to stop by, fat chance with me. I just had a busy day; my PC is in slow motion and on top of that more than 200 messages in 1 day? I thought I was hallucinating. I had 2 pinch myself 2 realize that I was awake, hahaha. Plizzzzzzz send me Pookie, maybe she can help me replying 2 the messages, would you? I promise that she will be back to you thinking about how wonderful the pottery video was, hahahaha . . .
I have 2 keep going, 2 more pages to go and then I retireeeeeeee to the good life my friend, to my beddy bed . . . Many kisses and terracotta hugs!!!
M@risol

Well Marisol if you're not hallucinating than you're back on the Cherry again, hahahaha

Marisol, people always ask me why do they call mc the love man, well besides bedding countless women, I am a con man by trade. I can sweet talk any lady out of her savings and their clothing but she has to have one or more of the following requirements: Money, more money, gorgeous, and good in the sack, I'm not a greedy man per say, but she's got to give me some, no besides that, money and if she's rich, more money. By gorgeous I mean a body to kill for, 36, 24, 36 is dandy but not my only candy, hahahahaha. Enjoy Perez Prado, ciao, J.
Perez Prado—Cherry Pink and Apple Blossom White

Wowwwwwwww, what nice music you got going on. Perez Prado the Cuban Mambo guy yeahhhhh. Lucy I'm home . . . . hahaha :):)
I'm super late, I had a hectic kind of day, but it's better late than never and here I am to wish you a wonderful night and bug you a little bit more . . . . hahaha . . .
All the best 4 you and hope everything is under control on your side, hahaha
Many kisses and hugs . . .
T.G.I.F . . . . Yeapppppppp, Meeeeeeeeee, M@risol

Girl I'm your good and plenty, your sugar cane, your honey dew, and I'm going to more than lick you up, cos you're my candy on a stick, taste you inside out from head to toe, and rock you good, make your body tremble with delight so get ready cos here I come. Let Mtume tell you some more, Jimmy. Ciao and how, hahahaha . . . .
Juicy Fruit—Mtume

Have a great day sweet juicy fruit man . . . . hahahaha
❀غـ7ﺭﻭ,I Wish 4 "you"

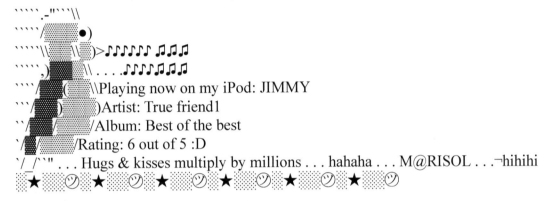

⟨≟⟩Great start 4 Monday
⟨≟⟩No obstacles 4 Tuesday
⟨≟⟩No stress 4 Wednesday
⟨≟⟩No worry 4 Thursday
⟨≟⟩Smile 4 Friday
⟨≟⟩Party 4 Saturday
⟨≟⟩& great fun 4 Sunday
Much love and happiness 4 you sweetie . . . . M@risol

Wow you always make me feel special and loved with your gifts. I wish I could reciprocate but I'm not artistic with a pen or a computer. But if you were here I would show you how good I am in so many other ways. No, I can't sing so that's out of the question but I'm good at everything else, don't ask hahahaha. Hey is that a drawing of the Dodo Bird. I have a bunch of them at my work place, they are not only lazy but ugly, uggghhh don't ask . . .
Jimmy, Mr. Wonderful

Your BG is totally impressiveeee, Jimmy. One day I'm gonna die laughing so hard and who do I have to blame for it? Ummm, you guessed it right, U. I like pink roses and my favorite music is 'The Girl From Ipanema.' I advise you on time in case it happens . . . Hahaha . . . Have a super duper night and a SUPERCALIFRAGILISTICO Saturday . . . . Uffffm I said it . . . . Hahahahaha . . . . I'm out laughing all the way Pink Panther . . . Opppssss so long, good bye . . . Aloha, multiples kisses and you behave . . . This beach could be dangerouss. M@risol

Marisol I got to tell you a secret I'm a professional auditioner, I audition for anything and everything, ok so my batting average is .052. Well when this movie was in production I too auditioned for the lead part, yep I wanted to be LSD cos that's my favorite choice of drugs, shhh I kicked that habit years ago but I rather not talk about this here, they put me away but then I've been put away many times before. Well sad to say I didn't get the lead but I was an extra you can see me in the bar room scene hahahaha, hey I got so drunk they tossed me out the door, so half a part is better than no part, enjoy the movie scene, byeeee
J, the artist formerly known as the love man
The Audition—The Producers (1968)

Uuuuuuuu, I see the auditioner is back in business, hahaha. Oh gush well I know I'm gonna finish my night rolling on the floor cos of you my good and sweet friend. Your stories make headlines around your country. You are gonna be as famous like the Pink Panther or perhaps Sherlock Elementary Watson, elementary, jajaja..¬..

Have a super duper night and please behave and say hello to Pookie . . . Hokkie . . . Hookie Pookie . . . .

besitos,

M@risol

"Oh gush," hahahaha what the heck is that??? An oil well or what, hahahaha, jew so fun knee!!! Yes I am Sherlock, last name Holmes and I'm looking for an Elementary Watson of my own. What are her qualifications she's got to be creative, spontaneous, and a little devil. Like when we go to the beach we go into the water skinny dipping. What is skinny dipping, hahahaha letting it all hang out, fuhgettaboudit we'll be the popsie twins, red all over and the center of attraction, me with my big head and you with your pretty . . . . well you know hahahaha;

J, aka Mr. Naughty But Nice

Hellooooo sweetie I'm running so late tonight but well here I am to wish you a lovely and romantic night with your kitten . . . . hahaha . . . . opppps Your comment about my video was out of this world . . . . I love it dear and yes you are gonna laugh a lot about what happened 2 me but I will tell you tomorrow. I'm kind of tired; I had to respond to so many messages that my fingers are almost numb, hahaha. I need a secretary. I told you the other day "The Girl Of Ipanema" is my favorite song of all times, maybe I was born in the wrong country. It should have been Brazil, hahaha and the "Samba Pa' Ti" with Santana, hahaha. Many kisses from your NUTTY friend, not naughty . . . . Okay, hahaha

Solecitoooo

Hey I can be your secretary but I get extra perks. What extra perks, I take a siesta after breakfast and lunch, and I need a massage to get the kinks out of me. I have wild parties at my house every night and my body takes its toll of bruises from them girls, they like it rough. No we don't play ping pong or hop scotch our games are more physical. We mud wrestle and it's always two against me and the winner gets their wish, omg I let them win cos they then get their wishes, they have their way with me, hahahaha. Hey do you know how to wrestle, good then come on over and see if you can knock me down and if you win you can knock me down again and again ahahahahha Bye bye you sexy thing you,

J

I knew, I knew that you would love that story about the incident that happened to me with my friends from there. It was so funny for me that every time I tell my friends or other people they roll on the floor laughing. I should be a standup comedian, hahaha. I have it in my blood running from up and down my mitral and vitral heart valve, hahaha I sound like a heart surgeon, how crazy I can be? I can assure something with me, you never get bored!!! If it's not one thing after another . . . sometimes I feel like a hurricane, a big Tsunami, a tornado, an earthquake, all that together . . . Imagine that? The end of the world before 2012 . . . . hahaha

M@risol

Oooooo weeeee you sound like fun, I would never get bored with you, please, please let's get this party started. Good god woman where you been all my life, I can't wait till we get together, is that a one on one or you invite your girlfriends over to watch and do they participate in your games. I love women who are crazier than me and love rough games. Don't worry about my heart I can take anything you got. So how tall are you and how much do you weigh, why I ask, don't ask ahahahahaha, Love you pudding pie . . .
J, the artist formerly known as the love man

ahaaaaaaaaaaaa 65/35 . . . . 65% for me smarty boy and 35% for you, jajaja . . . It seems that you like the story from earlier today and it's a true story. It really happened but it was such a good idea for me, jajajaja . . . U can't resist eating for free at restaurants . . . . U made me laugh when I read it on my channel, jajajaja . . . . I have to charge 65% cos it's all my idea. U just give the finishing touches, the corrections, jajajaja. You are funny sweetie, both of us will be a lethal combination. We would be an earthquake in NY . . . . rumblinggggg . . . hahahha . . . A good laugh is healthy and keeps you happy . . . . So I'm glad I made you happy another day . . . Muchos besitos chico lindo y I see you later. Love you my naughty boy
M@risol

Yes folks I must give credit where credit is due, it was Marisol who gave me the idea for the roach stories when she experienced it herself. You see she was out and about enjoying the good life, you know wining and dining like there's no tomorrow, let me explain. While having a drink she spotted a roach clinging to her ice cube in her glass and that was the beginning of my roach schemes here's one of them, oh yeah I revealed half a dozen. I guess when you got it you flaunt it, no not that, check this one out below:

Folks I got a story to tell you, you remember when I tried to scam restaurants for a free meal by planting roaches in the food they were serving us well I got away with it 25 times but got caught once and here's what happened on my 26th attempt. I took Pookie and four of our best friends to a fancy restaurant in NYC. Well we ordered the best and two bottles of Dom Pérignon. Oh we were having a swell time, dancing, eating, drinking, and laughing when all of a sudden the roaches in that little match box came lose in my suit jacket, all twelve of them as I was dancing Them critters were crawling all over me and I was itching uncontrollably and started to dance the jitterbug in hopes they would all come out. The folks at the tables were starting to clap for me, I guess I was dancing up a storm they thought I must have been Fred Astaire reincarnated. Pookie looking so surprised and unable to catch up with me looked so happy for me but when I whispered in her ear about the roaches she jumped back and started to laugh uncontrollably but from a distance. Then I noticed the roaches were falling to the ground then I did a Sammy Davis Jr. tap dance routine only to stomp them critters to death. I was smoking hot with my tap dancing and I did manage to kill all but one. When the owner heard and saw my performance and the folks clapping and giving me a standing ovation he took the bill and tore it up and said I should come again. Well I did achieve my goal, a free meal. Well the moral of the story let Pookie hold the roaches and one or two roaches should be more than enough a dozen is way too much, enjoy this Leo Sayer song, he too knows how to get a meal for free, hahahaha,

Ciao J, the artist formerly known as the love man
Leo Sayer—Long Tall Glasses

Your new story is a knockout hahaha, so the roaches made you dance the lambada, cha-cha . . . . tango, break dance. No wonder the owner wants you back U are gonna be The Entertainer. Like the song your stories are so funny and familiar to me, ummmm where did I hear that before? Those roaches, ahhhhhh, hahaha. Well sweetie I hope you still dancing, tapping, jumping . . . whatever but be happy, that's right, beeeee what you wanna beeeeeeeee, like a Busy Bee, hahaha . . . . Good night my sweet friend and hope to see you tomorrow :):)
Kisses and much love sweetie
M@risol.

Marisol, I think you are getting senile; no I didn't do the lambada or the cha cha, or the tango or break dance. I said I did the jitterbug and a tap dance routine, weren't you listening to the words that were coming out of my fingertips. You sure are funny and a bit slow, but then that's why I love you so, you take my stories and make me bigger than I am. From a mole hill you make me to be a mountain, yes Mount Jimmy, taller than Mt Everest or Mt. Kilimanjaro. Love you girl and thank you once again, ahahaha. You are slower than molasses and yet pretty as a flower,
J

Folks I got some bad news and some good news to tell you. Remember that incident when Pookie and I went to the restaurant and we found a roach attached to an ice cube in her drink and how all the charges were dismissed and they gave us another free dinner on them to boot. Well here's the good news for the past fifteen days we've been eating at some of the finest restaurants in NYC, breakfast, lunch, and dinners and drinking Dom Pérignon. How did we do it, sushhhh we brought along our own roaches hahaha. Oh I don't have any at home I paid a fella five dollars to bring me some for his troubles. Now here's the bad news I took a bunch of us to an Italian restaurant and when I confronted the waiter with the roach in Pookie's drink he immediately called the owner who upon hearing my complaint grabbed me by the collar and said I would be dead meat if I didn't pay up roaches or no roaches Well lucky for me a cop passing by saw us scuffling and took me in to the courthouse where the judge hearing what had occurred ruled that I had to pay or work it off. Well since my books aren't selling to well lately I took the work detail offer. I have to wash dishes, and pots & pans every weekend for Mr. Don Corleone for the next 6 months or he would make me an offer I couldn't refuse, no not the judge Mr. Don Corleone. Hey how was I to know the late Godfather had a grandson. Oh well my scam was good till it lasted. Moral of the story don't fecking mess with the mob, roaches or no roaches. Enjoy the movie clip, ciao J, the artist formerly known as the love man
Marlon Brando—I'm Gonna Make Him An Offer He Can't Refuse (from 'The Godfather')

Investigation Departemente here . . . FBI, CIA, INTERPO, KGB, PINK PANTHER and last but not least, SHERLOCK HOLMES, there is an ongoing investigation going on to know who's that Pookie Girl Jimmy always talks about. Open case until further notice, hahaha, just kidding . . . U know me it's just a nonstop laugh sweetie and you know I always be

your friend no matter even if I have to send the entire investigative departments around the world . . . hahaha . . . . bottom line is that I care and your friendship is special and important 2 me . . . . Capito Don Corleone? Should I call the Mob too . . . ummmmm. Many kisses and much love sweetie, and please never ever change for the 10,000th time. hahaha
M@risol

Hey my Pookie Girl is so shy she doesn't want her identity be known for fear she might be kidnapped. You see she knows how much I love her and if she were to be kidnapped she knows I would do anything to have her back dead or alive. She's my one heart's desire, the apple in my eye, the trophy on my pedal stile. I really must thank her cos she's looking out on my behalf. So Marisol let's keep this on the download, you know not mention her or do anything to discover who she is. Let's just say this is the secret of the century, only I know her identity, oh and her too hahahaha.
J

Marisol while we're on the subject I got a confession to reveal that will astound you believe it or not I'm really a midget, we don't like to be called that, we prefer small people, no different than u or your kids. You see God created all types of people & we are proud, we're invincible & if you ever see me walking down the street, call me Jimmy or Jockomo, my wrestling nick name, but never midget cos then I'll have to body slam you & hurt you. Hey enjoy Randy Newman, that big jerk. Byeeeeeeeee,
J, aka Jockomo
Randy Newman—Short People (1978)

Hey Jackomo, you have 2 comb your hair a little better, I don't like spiky hair . . . . hahaha . . . Youuuuu and your messages make me laugh so hard . . . . Sew when are you gonna get your tattoo with my name? I want to see that, hahaha. I hope you wax your chest first . . . . otherwise you are gonna look like your picture in the bottom of your page . . . hahaha :):)
Well the bottom line is, I always get a kick out of you. Never change sweetie coz you are 2 funny and your sense of humor is endless, hahaha. U always come out with the craziest ideas that make everybody cracking up starting with me of course. Have a delightful and hilarious day Jackomo and I'll be waiting for you . . . the dance and tattoo, hahaha. Bit it . . . . Bit it . . . . Bit it . . . .
hugs & kisses . . . Jackomo style
Mrs. Jackomo . . . .

Bit it . . . . Bit it . . . . Bit it . . . . Say what???? Hahahaha and who the heck is Jackomo, its Jockomo, you silly goose hahahaha
J

Marisol I got a story to tell you that you just ain't going to believe, do you know what Mickey & Minnie, Romeo & Juliet, Samson & Delilah have in common with me, well when we get to making love it's like a five alarm fire cos we are so hot something's bound to burn. Omg you can fuhgettaboudit cos nothing is going to cool us down no how. You

know what they say, you fight fire with fire, but then that's another story for another day in the meantime enjoy the Pointer Sisters who will tell you some more, ciao,
J, the artist formerly known as the love man
Pointer Sisters—Fire

Btw call all the Fire Departments around your neighborhood, it seems that your fire is gonna be hugeeeeeeee, fuegoooooo, fireeeeeeeeee, somebody call the Pink Panther, hahaha
One million besitos 4 you,
Solecito, M@risol

Your messages are always enchanting and funny 2 the max that's why I pressed the wrong buttons now I'm laughing hysterically. OMG don't worry I know where to come if I have to find the beautiful creature with spiky hair . . . . hahaha . . . . ET go home or Chucky?????
Hihihh, I love it . . . :):) M@risol.

ET and Chucky, hey by any chance are you comparing me to those two creatures from out of this world, they aint got nothing in common with me. Now if you had said, Arnold, or Rocky, or Clint now that would put me where I should be, a macho handsome devil. And my stories are not intended to make you laugh, it's just my autobiography of the man I am, tall, handsome, charismatic, giving, Guinness record holder, and now a world renowned author. Wait till I write about you oooooooo weeeeee it's going to be a Triple X-rated book about your adventures hahahaha. Well if you want me not to reveal the dirt on you, you got to take care of me ahahahaha I know, I know I'm too much, that's what the ladies always say hahahahaha,
Bye bye,
J

Folks, here's a story that Marisol told me in confidence and I want to share it with you. A couple was planning to get married but the woman had some sexual encounters before that her fiancé didn't know about. So she heard about this surgeon that performs some type of surgery to make you brand new again, you know, like a virgin by using a tympanic membrane from the ear. She went to see him and was convinced that this would fix the problem. The surgery went off well and the doctor told her to see him in six months. The six months passed and she went to see the doctor. He anxiously asked how was everything and she responded: well Doc. everything is fine except there's one problem, when my husband whispers in my ear I have to raise my leg, hahaha, enjoy Like A Virgin by Madonna, ciao and how,
J, the artist formerly known as the love man
Madonna—Like A Virgin

Oh you sure know how to tell a story, don't forget my cut 65 for me and 35 for you. Well this was my story I need to be rewarded for what I say not what you heard ahahahaha
Love you Jimmy Boy
Mari you know what

Folks I once had a sweet heart who rocked my world, this Freddie Jackson song reminds me of her. What became of her, oh why are you doing this to me, she ran off with another fellow, yep she became a nun, I guess she had a bigger calling and I was small fish compared to him. So in honor of her memory I dedicate this song to her, I think she's on the other side of the globe somewhere taking care of real business,
J
Freddie Jackson—Rock Me Tonight (For Old Times' Sake)

The best thing you can do my friend is open a convent and get your nun back, maybe after few years . . . you are the Big Fish now . . . . hahaha. Ok I Got 2 Go swimming back on the Atlantic . . . wish me luck :):) . . . Call the coast guards just in case . . . hahaha:):)
Miss M

A CONVENT!!! That's not the house I want to open up or run, something with more meat to it hahahaha, are you available and what's your going price ahahahahaha
J

You know it is true I am priceless, and you should start paying me for my services. What services you ask, for making you laugh and for my added bonuses I give you. Well I can't mention them here; You Tube would kick us out for solicitation, ahahahahaha. Enjoy The Animals, they too have a house they like visiting . . .
Ciao J, aka Master Jack
The Animals—House Of The Rising Sun

Hahaha . . . . you are crazy, I'm rolling on the floor laughing. Thank god I have my PC on the floor. I'm not talking about Jenifer Lopez song (On The Floor) is the real floor . . . . hahaha. Hey instead of Ms. Universe how about JANE? Who could be Tarzan? And Chitaaaaaa . . . hihi . . . . well don't worry I Will Survive. Just bring Gloria to sing the song and everything is under control . . . . grrrrrrrrrrrrGGGG¬RRRRR . . . . grrrr . . . the Leonesssss is out of the Bird Cage . . . . pardon me . . . The Lion's Cage . . . . byeeeeeeeee . . . alohaaaaaa . . . hahaha.
Fondue from Melting Pot . . . . ttttttttttttttttttttttt
M@risol

Well I was just thinking we can play the parts of Tarzan and Jane, we're both hot and saxy why not, and it'll expand our horizons. Who knows maybe we'll audition for that Spanish Patient movie, and you just know I will blow you away with what I got in up my sleeves. We'll send the camels to bed and I'll ride you like a camel hahaha or you me depending who's on top of the situation, don't ask hahaha. This is for you my Candy cane. It's XMAS In June, hahaha:):)
♥you are the STAR to my BURST,♥
♥you are the M to my M&Ms,♥
♥you are the POP to my TART,♥
♥you are the MILKY to my WAY,♥
♥you are the FRUIT to my LOOP,♥
♥you are the LUCKY to my CHARMS,♥

♥you are the ICE to my CREAM,♥ but mostly . . . .
♥you are the BEST to my FRIEND♥ and keep in touch. Otherwise no more candies . . . kisses . . . . M@risol

Hahahahaha, you are delightful, I just can't imagine my life without you, you always give me surprises and lots of goodies, I think I love you but let's keep this between us, no need to tell the world, and besides I got Pookie and you got, you got, heck you got somebody and he better be good to you or I'll come there and hurt him good. Bye bye Pumpkin,
J, the artist formerly known as the love man

Marisol I need your opinion on something, when I meet a woman for the first time is it proper to ask her to let me paint her toe nails and then she paints my toe nails and then we go out and paint up the town. Why I ask cos I'm smitten by this pretty young thing, she's got the prettiest brown eyes and when she walks, she wiggles, and when she talks, she giggles, she just drives me wild. Oh what am I to do, so that's why I ask you for your advice, thanks Honey Bunch, so are we on hahahahaha,
J

Hey sweetie your messages always make me laugh, you are one of a kind Jimmy . . . . Please bring more nail polish you are running out, hahaha:):) . . . . Love it, love you. This is hot . . . hot . . . hot . . . . oleee . . . oleee . . . oleee hahahaha!!!!!! Hugs & kisses and be good Johnny, pardon me, Jimmy, jajaja
M@risol

Hellooooo Hammer Time . . . hahaha, you crack me up with your messages and videos. Why you don't have a show on TV? It will be a big hit I guarantee you that. I will be the first one in line to get in the studio, hahaha. U just let me know and I'll make my airline reservation with enough time to get there . . . many hours and ocean in between, hahaha. I don't want 2 go swimming is gonna be 2 exhausting for me, hahaha. Well sweetie I really enjoy all your comments, stories, videos, everything makes my day happy and wondering what will be next? Ummmmm always good and funny. Have a gr8 night and keep that smile from ear 2 ear . . . and by the cute cat . . . miauuuuuuuuu!!!!!!!
M@risol

Folks we interrupt this program with breaking news, Barcelona lived up to the hype last night at Wembley Stadium, brushing aside Manchester United in masterful fashion, securing another Champions League title and cementing their legacy as the greatest team of this—or perhaps any—era. The final score was 3 to 1. The Spanish Soccer Armada was invincible so 3 cheers for Barcelona is in order, hip hip hooray, hip hip hooray, hip hip hooray. I personally know one little gal over there who's jumping for joy as we speak so I raise this glass in her honor. Ok, ok but can their armada beat the USA in baseball, or basketball no can do, hahahaha. Enjoy Queen, thanks J, the artist formerly known as the love man
Queen—We Will Rock You / We Are The Champion

Very good announcement for our Futbol Champios . . . . FC BARCELONA . . . . Yesss . . . Well done my friend I appreciate your gesture and maybe one day will be basketball too. As a matter of fact we play basketball here and not bad, not bad at all . . . . hahaha
Happy Sunday friend kisses and hugs 4 you!!!
M@risol

Your description was very funny as everything else you send me. I told you, you are better than going to a PSYCHOLOGIST. Just a laugh session on your channel and you are cured 4ever, jajajaja . . . . your video is hilarious . . . it's a laughing all the way, jajajajajaja . . . . You take care and keep your sense of humor all the time: D
hugs & kisses
M@risol

I don't know about psychologist but I do know I know how to cure what ails you. I am a lover by nature and most women need what I got, sometimes they throw themselves at me and being a gentleman I shower them with kindness hahahaha Well that's what I call it, U may have another name, love session, seduction, or a jump in the sack. It's all the same, I seduce them and make the woman come out of them, and you don't want to know. My methods are unique and mouthwatering good. Hey if you would like a sample make an appointment with my secretary and we'll get together and I'll drive you mad hahahaha, Well you can call it what you want but when I'm through with you, you will go mad, hahahahaha, so long sweet lady, Jimmy has left the building ahahahaha
J

Jajajaja . . . your featured vid is just 2222222222 funnyyyyyy and your message is even better, thank God I'm a happy person, but if I were one of those depressed ones here in Ytube I will come to your channel and laugh until I die, jajaja. Your humor is amazing and sharp like one of those good German knives jajaja, please never change, continue like that and make us happy like a frog when it's raining. Ummmmm I'm singing in the rain . . . lalalalalaaaa, oppppsssss I better go and keep replying on some messages . . . . good bye . . . so long . . . aloha . . . ciao . . . adios . . .¬. hasta la vista baby . . . I'll Be Back!!!
Much love & hugs
M@risol

Oh there's no need to thank me, it's an honor and besides having you will make me shine cos my friends will see I got good taste in Hotties. Just do me a favor, no flirting with anybody but me or I cut you lose like a goose, a long necked one at that . . . . ahahahaha
J, the artist formerly known as the love man

OMG . . . you are 2 much Jimmy . . . . I can't stop laughing with you but my recommendation, go and see a psychiatrist and later the fortune teller, and by the way I'm not a gypsy but I have a crystal ball and I can tell you your future . . . hahaha. I better I can hardly type hahaaaaaaa¬hahahaaa
M@risol

superlatina0582 OMG Jimmy I agree with Marisol . . . youuuuuuu are too much you are very funny! But I love it!

I guess when you got it liked I got it, all the girls want it hahahaha, yes I am too much!!!!! Hey, how did she know that, hummm. Marisol, are you spreading my personal info hahahaha!!!!
J

Marisol it's true so help you god I once had a Black Magic Woman, oh lordy lord you don't want to know, she drove me insane. She mesmerized me to death. I dreamt of her 24/7, eight days a week. I mean I couldn't get enough of her she was everything a man could want. Hot like an oven, sharp like a pistol, pretty as a daisy, good god in heaven. What became of her, she joined the circus and now shoots out of a cannon. Broke my heart the day the circus came into town. See I told you that you weren't gonna believe this, enjoy the song, thanks
J
Santana—Black Magic Woman

Helloooooo My Sweet Friend U thought that I forgot you, no way Jose or is it Jimmy or Mr. J hahahaha. I had a very busy weekend and struggling doing many things at the same time and going out and having some fun after such a hectic week in You Tube for me. I guess it was a full moon and all the crazy and creepy people were out and stopping by my channel . . . hahaha
M@risol

Marisol you have to be careful out there when there's a full moon. I meet all kinds of people who turn crazy and it's the fault of that full moon, no it's true. Let me tell you an incident that happened to me just the other day but I want you to promise me you won't repeat this to anyone else. Pookie and I were drinking and we ended up in a fight, no not a physical confrontation kind of fight, a hard feeling kind where we weren't talking. I mean she was so upset with me that she threw my clothes out the window and to make matters worse she ripped my clothes to shreds but I didn't realize that until I went outside to fetch them and here I am stark naked sneaking out to get my clothes and that's when she locked the door on me. I was so embarrassed the next morning as I awoken lying in the grass and all the folks staring and laughing at me. The next day it's no longer a full moon and Pookie welcomes me back with full arms as if nothing had ever happened. Wow, now tell me this, has that ever happened to you, hope not. Well enjoy this video by Jimmy Stewart from 'It's A Wonderful Life.' Remember mums the word . . .
C ya, Jimmy
Jimmy Stewart—It's A Wonderful Life

Jimmy I was debating so hard to close my channel or at least has it not visible. I was sick and tired of all this but you know I re-think many times and my real friends like you don't deserve that I go because I know your friendship is pure and sincere and I would feel terrible leaving the channel and my true friends . . . .

I just want to thank you for being so wonderful & caring to me Jimmy. U are one of those friends like a gem, like a diamond in a coal mine. You are amazing sweetie and I don't want to lose you for anything in the world so I'll stay put for you and all my good friends . . . M@risol

Wow, Marisol I can't imagine 'You Tube' without you. Let me thank you for not doing the unthinkable, closing your shop, you know, your channel. Yes you are right, all your friends will miss you and I would cry myself to sleep every time I come to your channel and it says, gone fishing hahaha, well you know what I mean, gone like closed shop and moved away. Heck we were just getting to know one another and already you're thinking of killing me with your absence, cos that's what I might have to do, kill myself if you go away. I couldn't bear to live alone without you. Pookie is just not enough for me, I need you like oxygen in my lungs, or blood in my veins, or a pool stick needs a cube ball, or like a kiss for the very first time or is it a virgin for the very first time. Ok ok you might as well know I'm a virgin, but don't blabber this to no one cos everybody thinks I'm a player, well got to go it's time for the porno movie of the week, I think it's "Debbie Goes To Washington," or is it Dallas, well some shit, bye bye and don't ever think of that again. In fact call me, or come on over so I can make your pain go away. I have the hands on treatment that will make you happy and drive you mad at the same time, don't ask . . . I love you girl yes I do, byeeeeeee Jimmy, The Handy Man, enjoy Paul Young, he too will miss you if you go away!!!

Re: Alohaaaaa Jim Carey is so funny no matter what character he plays. I love the Mask movie. When he sings Cuban Pete, jajajaja. I featured in my channel not too long ago, he's fantastico. When it comes to comedy and funny stop, Jim is the best . . . And Yesssssss I can imagine you looking like Marshall Bill with your hand on fire. Hahaha. is gonna be difficult to do pottery with one hand, ajajajajaja M@risol

Marisol I do remember when you had it featured on your channel that's when I realized you were off your rocker hahahaha and btw why you always imagining me getting hurt or on fire. Don't you love me, I love you and all I imagine is you looking hot and saxy. We are going to be the best duo ever, we'll write books, comedy sketches, and maybe even sing, but let's not think of me getting hurt okey dokey Missy. C ya later gator, after a while crockadile . . . . Jimmy-O

Marisol lately Pookie and I have been watching those big name romance movies but not just watching them reenacting the parts. Ok so I didn't fair too well with 'The English Patient' but I did score just the same if you recall hahaha even though Pookie was out cold, well when I try this 'Ghosts' love scene ain't nothing going to stop me unless we get electrocuted in the process, don't remind me. Tomorrow maybe 'Gone With The Wind' "FRANKLY DEAR I DON'T GIVE A DAMN" yep that was me doing Clark Gable, hahaha I always wanted to say that and then 'Casablanca' "HERE'S LOOKING AT YOU KID" right again me doing my Humphrey Bogart imitation and then "Lois & Clark" and then "Romeo & Juliet" and then, wooooo I'm already exhausted hahahaha how much loving can I go, hey wish me luck, ciao, Jimmy

Ps.

No auditioning required, hahahahaha, I got the part, J, the actor

Re: we should write a book together: Yes I read that the other day they split up. It's a shame cos they made such a pretty couple but you know being singers both of them living La Vida Loca without Ricky and all that, hahahaha. Is difficult, I can imagine being in the spotlight all the time and people following you, bugging you, aggravating you, OMG I rather be a NOBODY is easier that way . . . . So I have my paparazzi's under control when I go out. I wear a black long hair wig like you know who, noooo. like Lady Godiva and dark glasses and dress like Ellen DeGeneres, hahaha and where is Porta? How crazy is this? When you start writing on your channel combining with my messages is gonna be 3rd War World . . . BOOOMMM CATABOOOMMM . . . . hahaha . . . pure laugh 100% . . . . We are gonna be hired by SNL . . . . kind of Chevy Chase and I don't know any of the girls names . . . maybe you do . . . . hahaha . . . . Is gonna be . . . Funny Boney
M@risol

Hahahahaha why am I laughing, cos you say you wish you were a NOBODY, you are a nobody, ahahahaha. Changing the subject ahahahahaha Marisol I know we won't have any problems like J Lo and Marc Anthony cos I know you know that I am the boss, aka the head honcho. You see every gang has a boss, every corporation has a CEO, and every couple has a Ring Leader and that's me your Ring Leader. I will take care of you, buy you nice saxy dresses, pretty lingerie, and scnd you to the beauty parlor cos I want you to always look your best, pretty and saxy only for me, only the best for me. We will eat in the finest restaurants, no cooking for us. Do you like sushi, ummm ummm ummm, you will love your Ring Leader. Now I have to go out with the boys, so you stay home and get your beauty sleep. Do your exercises and say your prayers. See, who else loves you like I love you, nobody, I'm your one and only, your Ring Leader hahahahahaha. A nobody, ahahahahahaha ahahahahaha
Jimmy, aka Boss

Re: we should write a book together
U are right my friend we go together like Carrots n Peas . . . .
Like Forrest Gump and Box of Chocolates
Like Bonnie and Clyde . . . .
Like Cleopatra and Mark Anthony (not the singer cos I'm not J LO . . . jajaa)
Like Popeye and Olive Oyl . . .
Like Miss Piggy and Cookie Monster
All that and a bag of chips . . . ajajajaaaaa
M@risol

Funny once again, you're on a roll, not your kind of ROL, my kind of ROLL, you're so crazy but loveable, where am I gonna take you, NOWHERE!!!!! ahahahahaha Ummmm . . . . you like my sense of humor don't you Jimmy? hahahaha
We are quite the pear, Funny, Hilarious, Spontaneous, and Edible. All the right ingredients for a big success and good eating. And don't forget Charismatic . . . .

How about this title for our book . . . JIMMY AND CHIQUITA BANANA . . . . jajajaja . . . I'm not Carmen Miranda plzzzzzzzzzz, hihihihihi By the way I need to get something off my chest I notice something about you Jimmy, every time you share the profits is a killer 4 me. I'm not laughing, you always want the bigger chunk and I get the chocolate chips . . . It's not fair . . . . Let's do it the other way . . . hihihihihihh . . . I think that CYBER COMEDY will be funny, it has a ring, no a flair, hahahaha. And it's gonna be 50 50 and I mean 50 50, no expenses, no taxes, no excuses, split in the middle!!! I'm so happy to have a friend like you Jimmy . . . it's the chemistry (No lab) among us, so funny we are similar that what it is. :):)
Mari . . . .

Yes Marisol we will write my book ok, ok our book and yes I like the title already "Jimmy and His Chiquita Banana" OMG you are so right, we are similar, like day and night, like white on rice, sugar and spice, ham and eggs, butter on toast. You see Mickey had his Minnie, Brad his Jolene, Sonny his Cher, and I got you, my Chiquita Banana and when I get hungry I can eat you up, don't ask. Btw who the heck is Carmen Miranda hahahaha, only kidding, love her sombretto or what you macallit hahahaha. Don't worry Tutti Frutti I will share the profits down the middle less my expenses. What expenses you ask, hiring an agent to spread my name around, a chauffeur to escort me around, I don't do walking, and I need a private secretary to scratch my back and wherever else needs scratching, a valet for me so my clothes are ironed and I match properly, and all kinds of stuff so you will get what's left over, 22%. Hey 22% is better than no %, ok partner hahahahaha
J, fka the love man, Jimmy

Helloooo stranger:):) . . . Hey, your Pookie must be sooo lucky having a best friend like U . . .:):) . . . 1 in a million :). Well sweetie all the best 4 you and have a wonderful night and count all the stars before you fall asleep . . . sweet dreams :D kisses and much love. T.G.I.F . . . . hahaha :)
M@risol

Yes Pookie is lucky to have me and I'm so lucky to have you, hey I think this is a choo choo train hahahaha, thanks sweetie you're the best, love you . . .
Jimmy

I came with the LIMO 4 you and also a detective in case you need it. hahaha . . . Ohhhh boy :):) . . . Well sweetie your featured video is precious and very sweet . . . All your videos are always like that to make your female fans happy and Pookie 2 of course. Hey what kind of lounge is that in your BG? Ummmm . . . hahaha. Oh one of those :):) . . . I better go before I start joking around . . . :):) Many kisses and much love my sweet friend and remember the part, sharp like the knives :):) . . . hahaha T.G.I.F . . . . and you know what I mean :):) . . .
M@risol

Marisol I'm coming to your party wearing my white go-go boots and my hot pink spandex outfit. I want to be the hit of the ball. All your friends will be watching me and I will float like a butterfly and sting like a bee. Oh, those are your words hahaha, well I will be the center of attraction and everybody will know my name and who I am, Marisol's friend from across that big pond, yes from da Eu Es of Aye. Oh, I'll be on time and thanks for the limo

and I expect caviar and Dom Pérignon, nothing but the best for me hahahaha. I want to dance the Flamenco with you, got my boogie shoes packed and ready to go. We'll kill them dead with our Fred Astaire and Ginger Roger moves hahaha . . . Love you girl,
Jimmy aka The Hot Stepper, what I don't know there's no need to know

Naughty Boy . . . hahaha I hired 2 belly dancers . . . . U want her blond or brunette or both if you are greedy and hungry for some dancing in the moonlight, hahaha . . . .
Are you sure you can keep up with all these . . . remember that you have 2 c Pookie after that . . . and I don't want you 2 be running out of gas. Is there any gas station close 2 you hahaha? U are so incredibly funny and out of this world . . . that is a royal treat having you as a friend. Be always like that . . . crazy . . . funny . . . lovable, and charismatic XDD
Royal kisses flying thru the red carpet and reaching you . . . hahaha
Sol . . . . and get ready 4 tomorrow . . . I'll be here sharp like one of those German knives . . . . cutttttttttttttttttt . . . . hahaha
M@risol

Yes I want them both cos I want them girls to have some fun like Cyndi Lauper but this boy wants to have some fun too. I think it's called a ménage a tre or something or other, ooooooo weeeeee this is one party they will never forget, no you're not invited there's no room for four Good night Goldie Locks . . . hahahaha
Captain Jimmy Curt of the USS Enterprise signing out . . . .

My day was fantastic I went to the beach earlier . . . . but its soooooo hot . . . I lay down in the sand (but I didn't count the grains) for a couple of hours . . . . and to swim after that . . . . and now I look like an Oreo Cookie. Dark on the Outside and the marks from the bikini, white . . . . hahahaha . . . . Oh well that's what happens when you go 2 the beach. Maybe next time I will go to the nudist camp you and Pookie go too so I will get an even color tan, ahahaha
Have a super day sweetie and enjoy every second of your life, we only pass this way once in a lifetime or if you believe in reincarnation then perhaps dozens of times . . . .
Tons of besitos and don't be naughty . . . . jajajaja
M@risol

Marisol I sometimes go to the beach by myself, I let Pookie sleep so I walk on the shore and show off my manly physique you know, my beautiful body. The girls go wild, I see their lips dripping wet hahahaha, I know I'm too much for one woman, soon they're all walking next to me and they too are in their birthday suits and they ask me for the time and how's the weather. I think it's only an excuse to come rub shoulders with me. Rub shoulders, oh that means getting to know each other up close and personal. One girl wanted my picture; I said only if I get hers and her address. Why her address, in case the picture don't come out than I go to her house and do it again and again till we get it right. Hey let's not tell Pookie about this, what Pookie doesn't know, doesn't hurt her or me hahahaha. Hey in a previous life I was a slave to a princess I had to bathe her, and massage her from head to toe, she worked me to the bone, hahahaha no not that kind of bone you moron. What became of her, she was beheaded and so was I, don't ask but two heads were better than one and they did make a pair, hahahaha, Bye bye,

J, the love man, Jimmy

I haven't seen you sweetie. I think Pookie has kidnapped you somewhere in NYC . . . I have to call the CIA and FBI to see what's going on with you and Pookie . . . . hahaha . . . maybe you still at the beach counting the sand grains . . . . ahahahaha . . . . it's gonna be an endless job for you both . . . hihihih . . . Happy Saturday and my best wishes for you . . . Love ya :):):D
M@risol . . . alias T.G.I.F. (Thank God I'm Fabulous) . . . hahaha

No I wasn't kidnapped we were just keeping a low profile; we hibernate for days when it's that time hahaha. We close the windows, lower the shades, and put up that 'do not disturb' sign and freak out, hahaha don't ask. Hey, maybe you want to watch, it's going to cost you. Front row seating is a thousand dollars a pop and all the popcorn and ice cream you can eat is on the house but anything extra, booze, drugs will cost you another thousand. Oh btw I'm talking USD's that's right American currency no pesos, pesetas, yens, Euros, or pounds, heck not even Francs, Marks, or any of that Brazilian funny money and definitely no monopoly money either, now that's a steal hahaha. Hey you just might learn a thing or two or three, or maybe you want to partake, well that's going to cost you even more. What kind of guy do you think I am, I'm priceless and if you want some of this you're going to have to fork up, hahahaha . . . Bye, it's time for our full body massage event hahaha
Jimmy

The Bank Dick (1940) starring W.C. Fields as Egbert Sousè I am in your to do list, hahaha . . . U make me feel like homework. It's ok so get ready I will send my bill at the end of the month and don't worry it won't break your bank. Just a little enough to keep you alive and well, hahahaha . . .
U are funny and charismatic . . . U crack me up every time I talk to you . . . U never stop amusing me . . . Hahahaha . . . U are like that tabasco sauce . . . Spicy and ???? U figure it out I can't hahaha I can't stop laughing . . .
M@risol

Homework, did you say homework, I got plenty of homework for you. This week we're studying the anatomy of man, and next week of woman. Oooooo weeeee I always wanted to learn about the G-Spot on a woman. It is said if you touch the right spot on a woman she will be gushing a waterfall that can easily fill a barrel, now that I got to see up close and personal . . . hahahaha
J

U see how many ideas I gave you I'm endless resource of ideas. My brain is like a nonstop engine. Chooooo, Chooooooo. I'm smoking, not hot . . . Just my brand . . . . hahahaha. The Spanish Patient version would be a knockout. Spicy like a tabasco bottle plus some chilli peppers included. So get ready to call the fire departmento. This is going to be a huge fire of what? Love passion . . . Well something like that, hahahaha
M@risol

Wow, I can't wait till I do that movie, see it can only be one person for that role, no, not Tom Hanks, he aint Latino enough, heck he aint even Latino, but I am and also a hunk so you jes know I was born to play da part, now who will be mi leading lady, one guess hahahaha, you tell me you gorgeous saxy senorita, jajajajajaa, see I even laugh like a Latino macho man that I am got to go and rehearse, ciao Jaime, da Spanish Patiente hunko

U see I always contribute to your crazy ideas, I think we are very similar when it comes 2 that . . . Hahaha. 2 master minds putting thoughts together, a master piece to the best. How humble, Omg, U are excited about The English Patiente. The problem is you haven't seen "THE SPANISH PATIENTE" yet. It's even better and steamier, hahahaha. Just kidding)>). yep. Give me a smile plisss :D:D: M

No, but I will play the part and everybody will come see me at my best jajajaja ok ok see us at our best!!!
J, fka the love man, Jimmy

RE: sex scene from the English patient I'm dying laughing, are you sure he is not one of the Chipindale Guys? I would date him with the intensity he has and the Rainbow, hahahaha . . . It will be like "A RAINBOW CONNECTION" . . . . hahaha . . . . Omg I haven't seen video . . . Is 2 funny . . . The sound is a killer for goodness sake: D:D:D:D:D: M@risol
No I'm not one of them but I did try out as a Chippendale Dancer and they fired me cos I was too hottttttt, you know muy caliente in the sack or is it sacko grande or just sacko, ajajajajaja
J

Hahaha you are something else, coconut milk . . . . Is she a coconut tree? And you stay on the bottom until they fall on top of your face . . . . hahaha . . . Omg . . . I can't stop laughing with you . . . I'm sure that Pookie is gonna have the time of her life with you sweetie . . . . I can imagine.
I'm not like butterfly flirting with the entire YT . . . I have my virtual boyfriend . . . the others are friends that come to say hello or so but I'm pretty much steady in my relationships, is virtual but I'm faithful, believe it or not . . . don't laugh but it's true like a COCONUT TREE . . . and milk included . . . . ioppppsss . . . . Sunday is my day offfffffffffffffff . . . . ooooooooooffff
M@risol

Why do you laugh so what that I love milk, coconuts or what have you, it does the bones and body good hahaha. Fyi I used to date a girl who lived on a farm and she loved to give me her just squeezed milk. She was better than a cow, omg I couldn't get enough of her, don't ask hahahaha
J

U are marvelous sweetie . . . . you are so kind and nice to me . . . How I'm not gonna love my fun & caring friend? U always make me smile and happy every time I read you Jimmy . . . . U are like star dust . . . magic to me . . . plissss never change I told you many

times. U are gonna hear it more . . . hahaha . . . cos its true . . . . It's a blessing to have a friend like you that I can count on the good and the bad . . . that is what a friend is for . . . . don't worry about telling me who's Pookie I can figure it out by myself. I'm like Sherlock Holmes. Elemental Watson, Elemental . . . . hahaha . . . U don't know me yet . . . hahaha . . . in a good way Ok . . .:):)
The Divine Miss 'M'

Yes I am marvelous and so kind thanks for recognizing my attributes, well what am I getting in return that will have me smiling from ear to ear and that is music to my ears as well and in my heart and down my . . . Well you get my drift missy, you want this boy you got to give me something in return, milk for starters will do just fine but then I want it all hahaha. Don't mind me I'm just crazy hahahaha
J, fka the love man, Jimmy

Super-duper nutty reporting 2 you . . . . hahaha . . . . you are so funny Jimmy-O . . . your sense of humor is fantastic as well as your quality like Houdini to escape from questions . . . . not a real escape . . . haha . . . I asked U something yesterday and evade the answer . . . U just kill me laughing . . . . The Master of escape questions . . . oppppssss . . . . that's ok, it's just giving you a little bit of hard time . . . . is Tuesday why not? Especially after a long weekend for you its time 2 have your engines fired up . . . hahaha . . . Sweetie let me tell something . . . . don't say that you are like another friend and join the pack cos you don't have as many people in your channel . . . . U are a special friend 2 me . . . . it doesn't matter that I have many messages or friends in my channel . . . . I do have my special friends in that group . . . . and you are one of them . . . . so you are not gonna get lost in there . . . I just want 2 make sure that is not gonna happen 2 you . . . Okey Dokey?????
But is gonna cost you something . . . . hahahaha . . . .
M@risol

Thank you Marisol for those refreshing and most uplifting kind words, I'm so honored that you think of me as a VIP when it comes to you and so are you. Are you sure you don't mean R I P, oh well just as long as we're a part of each other's lives "Anything For You," yes it does sound like a song, the one by Gloria Estefan and do enjoy,
Jimmy
Gloria Estefan—Anything For You

Re: hello sweetie Ummmmmm . . . . I think your fireworks started earlier for the 4th . . . . I Want Your Sex . . . . hahahaha . . . U are a Naughty Boy . . . jajaja . . . I think your friend the one who made those sexy videos . . . . ummmmm inspire you 2 much . . . hahaha . . . . I can see the sparklers from here . . . you are like a rocket . . . Apollo 2011 . . . . oppppssss . . . . hahaha:):):D . . . Are you the Italian Stallion or the America/PR Stallion Stallion? Don't tell me you are Rocky Balboa . . . . let me see your smile from ear 2 ear :D——>like that!!!!!!!!!!!!!!!!
Well sweetie I just want 2 thank U for your nice comment about me . . . I'm gonna get to the point . . . that I'm gonna believe it that I'm like that . . . hihihihi . . . U are too nice to me and I appreciated 4 sure Jimmy-O . . . . I guess I'm 2 social and outgoing and people like that . . . . and what you see is what you get . . . In person I'm the same way . . . is a not stop

laugh . . . I'm glad U found me here cos we mix like Rum and Coke . . . let's call it Cuba Libre . . . Free Cuba hot drink . . . . or maybe we can be GIN . . .
M@risol

Hahahahaha whatever you got I want some, heck I'll even bottle it for a rainey day. You are so damn funny I just pee'd on myself laughing so hard. Where did you say you came from, you can't be from earth, you're too much, love it and I love you too hahahaha
Please be gentle with me, don't make me cry next ajajajaja . . . .
byeeeeeeeeeee,
J

☼my sweet master . . . room . . . . no pardon me . . . . master piece :_)
☼ "The whisper of the Universe is always all around U
☼ sending messages of love, peace, good vibes
☼ knowledge, understanding, harmony, joy . . ."
❤ ☮ :) ☼ ☾ ★have a great weekend sweetie and stay well. Kisses
M@risol (the brown eye girl) . . . . the other one . . . hahaha

Now you know why I got to have you as my partner in crime, and you will get your even share 50 50 or nothing at all, that's what you deserve and lots more, kisses and lots of hugs galore,
Jimmy, your better half, hahahaha

U are very smart Mr. Accountant . . . 65/35 . . . . no problem . . . I'll take the 65 and you get the 35% . . . . hahahaha . . . I love it . . . U are too funny and cute.
Have a great day and happy 4th of July over there . . . . save some ribs . . . corn on the cob and beans . . . but not much . . . . U know what happen with the beans . . . . The more you eat . . . . OPPPPPSSSSSS . . . . uuuuuhhhhhiiiii . . . . U get a flat tire, ahahahaha . . .
chiao bambinoooo, besitos,
The Divine Miss 'M'

Hahahaha flat tire, I thought you were gonna say something else, hahahaha you sure know how to make spicy up a story and ad lib as you go along. Yes you are spontaneous and deadly too, and you say I'm the crazy one, hahaha, it takes one to know one. Tell me Marisol, were you ever hospitalized for being fruity, you know, for being nuts. Well you could have fooled me cos you are nuttier than a fruit cake hahahaha. And I don't want some of your cake unless it's filled with cashew nuts cos those are my favorites, hahahaha. Well I better leave you so you can take your meds and your shock treatments; you deserve them and more than just a jolt. a mega para boom kilowatt is what you need . . . . Ciao, Jimmy

Thanks sweetie for thinking so high about me . . . . It's like flying a jumbo jet 747 at 30,000 feet high . . . . hahaha . . . . I love it . . . You are so sweet my friend that why I never . . . ever . . . I'll lose you . . . You are 2 precious and caring to let you go as a friend . . . not even 4 the Queen of the tube according to her . . . hahaha . . . wishful thinking . . . . oppppssss . . . Ohhh well I just want 2 let you know that I love and appreciate your friendship like a bag of . . . . not chips this time . . . . but a bag of 24K gold nuggies . . . . How about diamonds

or platinum . . . Well any ways you have no price . . . U are priceless my friend as simple as that . . . Many blessings, good wishes, and don't forget to post many messages on my channel and you will win all those prizes and an extra special for you? I let you pick it . . . . jajajaja good bye sweet master . . . . peace . . . . hihihh :):).
The other brown eyed girl. hahaha
M@risol

Wooooo hooooo and I get to pick it, you won't have to tell me twice what I want ajajajaja. Hey, you won't be sorry I'll drive you up a wall hahahahaha, bye bye, I like dreaming and so does, Kenny Nolan, enjoy the song . . . Jimmy

U won 3 prizes with me . . . . How lucky you are . . . . Omg!!!!!!!!

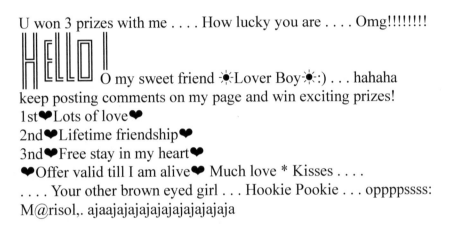 O my sweet friend ☀Lover Boy☀:) . . . hahaha keep posting comments on my page and win exciting prizes!
1st❤Lots of love❤
2nd❤Lifetime friendship❤
3nd❤Free stay in my heart❤
❤Offer valid till I am alive❤ Much love * Kisses . . . .
. . . . Your other brown eyed girl . . . Hookie Pookie . . . oppppssss:
M@risol,. ajaajajajajajajajajajajaja

Three prizes, omg I won the jackpot jajajajajajajaja don't ask!!!! What three prizes do you got and do I choose. I just hope it's edible don't tell me you got me some of your peaches or coconuts or your leg of lamb, ahahahahaha
J

Funny video . . . the best thing, don't wear anything, hahaha, just kidding . . . used the knot . . . . no . . . . no much better those panties, hahaha
gooooodddddd byeeeeeeeeeeee master
M@risol

Yeah I love this elevator commercial, and yes she wears them well, can't say that for the other ladies but "que se yo," Hey, I know more than you think jajajajajaja
J, fka the love man, Jimmy

Well I don't know if I'm witty or what, but spontaneous, YESSSSSS in capital letters . . . . Not a psychiatrist, I'm gonna be a psychologist. It has to be more with your behavior and the way you function inside society . . . . a psychiatrist is more for mental cases, depression, suicidal thoughts . . . both of them have an abroad range of interesting facts about human behavior ok tell me are you gonna make a story about a bag of chips with different flavors? . . . hahaha . . . I bet you will
M@risol

Well I will want to be your patient or is it client, well whatever "Book me Dano," hahahaha, A little bit of Hawaii Five-0, don't ask, Jimmy
Exile—I Wanna Kiss You All Over

Hahaha, you are crazy sweetie . . . U make me laugh so much with your stories, this piercing one is awesome . . . How you can come out with those ideas my friend? U are 2 much maybe a I have to talk to the brown eye girls 2 find out what's going on here . . . . jajaja . . . . U are my crazy boy. U are naughty and funny at the same time :):)
Thanks for sharing that beauty . . . . nice images and music :):) . . . . thanks a lot Jimmy
Double O-O
Solecito

Marisol you want to know the truth, I'm just not sure you can handle it, I carry a pencil in my pocket everywhere I go cos when I'm out and about if I see something funny I jot it down to remind me to expand on it and make it a whopper. What!!!!!, you never heard of a WHOPPER, no not that kind of a whopper, the hamburger kind hahaha, a made up story almost like a fib. Sometimes I forget to carry one, a pencil, and then I forget the idea and then I think and think and try to retrace my steps to try to get back that lost idea. Sometimes it works sometimes it doesn't well 'se la vie,' that's French for 'that's life.' Hey pretty soon I'll teach you to speak Americano hahahaha. Omg it'll be like teaching you bad words cos I say a lot of slang words, like fuhgettaboudit, gonna, wanna, omg you'll be like one of us but a hottie at the same time hahahaha . . . Hey I wouldn't want to change you, love you the way you are and do enjoy Billy Joel with his song, something tells me he's talking about you hahahaha
J

Ps
Peacock would be just the right thing I would love to eat and turtle soup, umm umm umm guess you'll be busy hunting for them ahahahahaha
Billy Joel—Just The Way You Are

Thanks sweetie 4 all the compliments that I don't deserve. I'm just a normal person with a funny bone, that's it. Maybe a comedian inside of me, who knows, I don't pre-make things. I write what I think at the moment. So what u see is what u get, quite a bargain, jajajaja. I'm not looking for Prince Charming or Mr. Trump, haha . . . I have a beloved one here and he's all that and a Bag Of Chips. Does it sounds familiar or I dreamed that? ummmmmm, hahaha
Have the sweetest dreams darling and all the angels from heaven will dance 4 you . . . . Ummm, It does not sound right maybe they play the harp & violin 4 you . . . . Oppppssss . . . nothing else my boy . . . . don't let your imagination fly in something else . . . :):)Good night . . . nite . . . nite . . . . Ms. Funny Bone is leaving . . . I have an important engagement with Morpheus . . . hahaha . . . . and he makes me sleep like an angel.
Angelical kisses . . . with wings included
M@risol

I agree there's something inside of you that wants to come out and do stand up, and sing, and dance, all the perfect ingredients for a comedy duo. Hey, let her out soon or I'll have to find another partner. I told all the TV networks we want top billing and top dollar, a million dollars each an episode, well after I take my expenses its 75 25. Hey 25 aint bad, it's still better than zero. So yes that's your cut, you are so lucky hahaha Hey I'll be back, going to see a man about a horse hahahaha

J

Re: wowwwwwww This is a good one, like Mohamed Ali, aka Cassius Clay.

Marisol: Float like a Butterfly and sting like a Bee . . . . jajajaja . . . that is a good one . . . I am as crazy as you, we make quite a team together . . . . sharp, quick minded and humorous . . . . what else can we ask? The perfect combination, we mix the 2 cultures and your book is gonna be the 2nd atomic bomb, jajajaja . . .

M@risol

Well I got news for her it's her book now too; she's the one who inspired me to co-write this book. Enough said enjoy the rest of the book . . . our book, our stories!!!

J, fka the love man, Jimmy

Re: Home Alone—Booby Trap Montage! This is one of my favorite movies for Christmas, is so hilarious . . . I like to call it "THE WET BANDITS" . . . . jajaja. I love the part when Joe Pesci's hair catches on fire and he sticks his head into the snow . . . ahahaha . . . and when the other guy is in the basement and all the power or whatever come from above and land on top of him and he looks like a ghost. Omg, my stomach hurts so much every time I watch it.

M'

Hey Jimmy this video is gonna knock your socks off; hahaha . . . . The anchor man in the back is so hilarious. He can't stop laughing the entire video. Everything wrong happens. The best part is at the end, I don't know how many times I've seen this video, but my stomach hurts every time I watch it . . . oppppsssss. That British accent is so funny and the guy trying to keep a straight face . . . but it's impossible, hahahha. Enjoy and please buy this vacuum, it's a bargain :) . . . . top of the line. hihi :D

hugs . . . . M@risol

Marisol you wanna know how many vacuum cleaners they sold, are you ready, are you holding on your hat, zero, zilch, nada, you got to be blind to buy one of those there utensils hahaha, that's what it is a utensil cos it can't pick up more than a forkful hahahaha. Now it would be false advertisement if they were able to sell that box of bolts to a blind man . . . . Don't tell me you bought one of them, than that means you're either blind or crazier than I thought, woo maybe you wanna buy the Brooklyn Bridge off of me, I'll give it to you half off, fifty bucks and that's a steal hahahaha, yes by me . . .

Ciao, Miss Gullible . . .

J, fka the love man, Jimmy

Conclusion

Well I hope you've enjoyed yourselves and you learned some valuable lessons in life. When you think about it, everybody has a story to tell. It can be written in a form of a tell all book or maybe as an autobiography if you have a lot to tell. Me just portions of my true experiences and of my fantasies. Hopefully, it will make me a killing when this book makes the New York Times best seller list. I don't know how my wives are going to take this? What am I saying!? They're going to want a share of the royalties and that'll leave me back where I started, penniless once again. Next time, I'll use a pseudonym. You know a pen name also known as a nickname to disguise myself and keep it all to me.

Was I right about my friend Marisol? Was she everything I said as being one heck of a woman? And yes, she writes like she speaks, and her comments are totally ridiculous. If you ask me, she isn't working with a full deck. But then again, she probably thinks that way about me. It goes to show, if we can be friends, the possibilities are endless for the rest of the world maybe end all wars.

Well it's time to go, working on next project. It's called 'games of my youth.' No it's not what you think. It's about all the games I participated when I was a kid from the age of 5 until I became a man, and had to put away my toys and go to work. Hope you haven't seen the last of me. Like Arnold Schwarzenegger I'll be back and with a vengeance, byeeeeeeeeeeee, Jimmy

About the Author

Jimmy Correa was born on a military base and grew up as an Army brat for the first eight years of his life. As a toddler, he and his sisters traveled the world all over. His father, a career soldier was a big disciplinarian man. Jimmy learned right away the importance of integrity, honesty, and respect. He bypassed the opportunity to attend college on numerous scholarships to work for a prestigious Wall Street firm for over 30 years. He then moved to North Dakota and briefly worked for an insurance company processing back office client changes requests. It was during this time he put out his first book. From that point on his confidence and workmanship improved more and more so he says. He moved back to NYC to live with his daughter who he thinks is not only a source of inspiration to him but is a whole lot funnier and definitely a better writer in her own. He's currently working on a half dozen or so other projects and claims there is not enough time in the day. Keep an eye on him, he is a man on a mission and won't stop till he completes them all.

Other books written by author Jimmy Correa